THE RED-STAINED DESERT

BRENT TOWNS
WITH
SAM TOWNS

ROUGH EDGES PRESS

ROUGH EDGES PRESS

The Red-Stained Desert

Paperback Edition
Copyright © 2020 Brent Towns, Sam Towns

Rough Edges Press
An Imprint of Wolfpack Publishing
5130 S. Fort Apache Rd. 215-380
Las Vegas, NV 89148

roughedgespress.com

All rights reserved. No part of this book may be reproduced by any means without the prior written consent of the publisher, other than brief quotes for reviews.

This book is a work of fiction. Any references to historical events, real people or real places are used fictitiously. Other names, characters, places and events are products of the author's imagination, and any resemblance to actual events, places or persons, living or dead, is entirely coincidental.

Paperback ISBN 978-1-68549-150-5
eBook ISBN 978-1-68549-149-9
LCCN 2022944113

THE RED-STAINED DESERT

CHAPTER ONE

Like an angry wasp trying to free itself from a spider web, the cell in Dave Nash's pocket buzzed violently. Somewhat distracted, he reached down to retrieve it, glancing at the screen momentarily before swiping the green phone to the right with a flick of his finger. Committed now to taking the call, he placed the black iPhone to his ear and murmured, "Yeah?"

"Nillahcootie," a distant voice said. "Four hours."

"Bullshit," Nash blurted out. "That's miles from fucking anywhere."

"Exactly. If you want the product meet us there with the money."

Lake Nillahcootie was on the Broken River in northeast Victoria. It was part of the Broken River system which flowed through Benalla before joining the Goulburn River at Shepparton. Like he'd said: miles from anywhere.

"OK," Nash sighed, sounding inconvenienced.

"Good. Don't be late. I mean if it's too much trouble—"

"No, no, it's fine," Nash replied urgently.

The line went dead, and Nash stared at the phone, his brown eyes taking in the dark screen before he lifted his head and looked at the woman across from him. Detective Sergeant Gloria Browning had her long blonde hair pulled back from her face in a severely tight ponytail. Nash stared into her blue eyes and for a moment said nothing. Close in age, the pair were now in their mid-thirties and had some things in common: their careers with the Australian Federal Police—Nash as an undercover; and their daughter Rachel, a precocious three-year-old, even though they were separated.

Nash shifted his gaze, slowly taking in everyone around them in the Lygon Street café. Gloria grew impatient, sitting up straighter and leaning her head toward him. "Well?" she asked in a low voice.

"Nillahcootie in four hours."

"The lake?"

Dave nodded. "That's the one."

She let out a frustrated sigh. "Shit, that's miles away from anywhere."

"There seems to be an echo. That's what I said."

Gloria nodded, a plan already forming in her head. "We'll have to coordinate with Benalla police."

"Yeah. Hopefully, this will be the end of it."

The case they were working together had been ongoing for the last three months. It involved the influx of millions of dollars' worth of ecstasy through the port of Melbourne; those responsible were an Irish family by the name of O'Malley.

Relatively new on the block, the O'Malleys had been in Melbourne for only two years, and within that time, had slowly but efficiently eliminated most of their competition in a gang war that had seen the streets running red with criminal blood. Those that remained in business did so only at the pleasure of matriarch Betty O'Malley, whose mood could change in an instant, signifying the end of another one.

Betty's offspring, Colin and Peter, were both a-grade arseholes responsible for more than their share of hits in the time they'd been in country. It was with these boys that Nash had set up the buy. He'd made a mistake in assuming they wanted to meet down at the docks; instead, they were taking him way out of the city to do the deal.

Now he held grave suspicions that his cover was blown, and they planned on wrapping him in chains and dropping him in the lake. Even worse, it would be dark when the meet went down.

Gloria seemed to read his mind, pushing away her coffee cup and picking up her handbag. "I'll get Leroy and Annie running point. They can fly to Benalla and coordinate with the locals there. They should arrive up there within a couple of hours by the time they get mobilized. We can enjoy the drive. I'll have them set up a couple of observation points with a good line of sight to the car park."

"What about Frenchy?" Nash asked. Frenchy was Craig French, a new member of their specialist team. Since the bust with the Armenians the previous year, the brass had decided that the services of a specialised team were essential for tougher jobs.

Gloria shook her head. "He can stay here in Melbourne and keep an eye on Betty. He's not ready for his big boy boots yet."

"Gotta let him off the chain sometime, you know?" Nash pointed out.

"My team, my rules, Nash. You know that."

"The boss at home and at work, huh?"

"Damn right."

Nash paid their bill and while he did so, Gloria made the call to Detective Senior Constable Leroy Mertens.

"What's up, boss?" he answered.

"We've got a meet in four hours up at Nillahcootie."

"The lake?"

"Yes. I need you and Annie to fly up to Benalla and coordinate from there. Once you're set, you're both to head out to the lake and set up a couple of O-Ps. Take the SIG MCXs with you just in case this all turns to shit."

"Yes, ma'am."

"And cut out the ma'am bullshit."

"Sure, Gloria."

"Let me know once you're in position."

"Copy that."

Gloria ended the call just in time to see Nash walking towards her. "All in order?" he asked.

"So far."

"Let's go for that drive then."

By the time they hit the bridge across Lake Eildon at Bonnie Doon, the sun was throwing its last hurrah on the western horizon. And well known for its changeability, the Victorian weather began turning to shit. It was cold out, and the wind had picked up, the trees beside the road bending as though a giant hand were forcing them to bow and scrape. It was a sure bet that the rain would break out before too long.

Gloria drove the VF Commodore as though she was late for an appointment, and more than once, Nash told her to slow down. Her response, "If I slow down any more, I'll be in reverse."

"I sometimes think that might be safer."

"Fuck you."

"More than once."

"Arsehole."

Her cell buzzed and Nash put it on hands-free. It was Leroy. "Speak to me, wise one," Nash said.

"We're all good this end," came the reply. "The Benalla cops are stationed about two kilometers to the north of the lake. Annie and I are already in position."

"You got a good line of sight?"

"Yes."

"OK. If anything goes wrong, you drop the first one your sights find."

"Copy that. How far out are you?"

"About twenty minutes, but the rate we're going it won't be anywhere near that," Nash replied.

Leroy laughed. "See you when you get here."

"Hope not," Nash said, and hung up.

The guideposts on the side of the road whipped by, the vehicle's headlights illuminating the reflectors in a blur. Ten minutes later they turned left onto the Midland Highway. Neither Gloria nor Nash spoke until they passed the second Mansfield turnoff.

"Listen," Gloria started, "if this goes south—"

"It won't," Nash said to her as he took out his Glock 19 and checked it over. Gloria carried the same weapon but hers was tucked under her arm.

"They're not going to be happy when they realize you've brought me along."

"Just stay in the car until I sort it out. I'll think of something."

Gloria nodded. "Try Frenchy again."

Nash took her phone and dialed a number. He put it up to his ear and was immediately told by automated message that his call couldn't be connected. Pulling it away from his head he sighed. "Same as before," he told her.

"I don't like it," she said to him.

"His phone is probably flat."

"If it is, I'll cut his balls off," Gloria growled.

For the most part Lake Nillahcootie is long and deep and runs beside the highway and beneath it in places. So it was obvious to them when they'd reached the southern end of it. Recent good rains had the catchment filled to more than half full. Nash called Leroy and told him that they were almost there.

"Looks like you'll be the first to arrive," Leroy told him. "I've seen no sign of the O'Malleys yet."

Nash ended the call once more and said, "They're not there yet."

"Maybe they're not coming," Gloria replied, checking her mirrors and speedometer.

"No. They'll be there. They think they're about to make three hundred grand. They're not going to pass that up." He felt reasonably sure of the accuracy of his statement.

"I guess time will tell."

Gloria slowed the car a few minutes later and indicated to make the right turn onto the narrow road which led down to the carpark at the water's edge. She stopped the vehicle and turned both the engine and the headlights off. It was suddenly eerily silent sitting there in the dark. Neither wore comms or wires. It was too risky, plus the O'Malleys were no fools. The first thing they would do is look for them. Which meant that the Glock would have to stay in the vehicle as well.

Nash put it in the console and Gloria said, "I wish you would take that with you."

"You know how this goes, Gloria. You've been a UC just like me. That's one of the first things they'll look for. That's why we have backup."

"I still don't like it."

Nash nodded and thought about their daughter. Since her birth, Rachel had become the centre of his world. He couldn't imagine her not being around. Nor Gloria for that fact. Although they weren't together, together, the time they spent in each other's company had brought them closer again.

The phone buzzed and this time it was Annie. "Heads up. You've got visitors."

Nash looked out the window and saw two sets of headlights pull off the highway and onto the narrow road. "Here we go," he said to Gloria.

They sat there watching as both vehicles pulled in but left their lights on even though the engines were shut off. They were both dark SUVs, Toyotas. Nash waited a moment longer and climbed out. As he did, Gloria said, "Be careful."

"I always am," he lied, but could think of nothing more reassuring to tell her at the time.

After he'd closed the door, Gloria reached down and grasped her cell. She hit a couple of buttons and said, "Can you both hear me?"

"Yes, boss," Leroy replied.

"Loud and clear, Gloria," said Annie.

"If this all goes south you know what to do."

Standing on the rough asphalt beside the Commodore, Nash noticed that the wind was bordering on cold which was creating an almost urgent need to piss—the chill or nerves, he couldn't differentiate but probably a little of both. Nash stopped at the front of the car and waited for the new arrivals to alight from their vehicles. After about a minute of waiting all the doors on the left Toyota opened. Out of it climbed Colin and Peter O'Malley. Both men, although not clearly evident in the dark, had red hair and were quite solidly built.

They walked towards the front of their vehicles and into the light, throwing long shadows across the parking lot. Behind them came two more men. Nash expected that both would be armed. It was reasonable to assume they all were.

"You're early," Colin said. "I like that."

"You told me not to be late."

The Irishman nodded. "What I don't like is that you

brought someone else along to our fucking meet."

Nash had heard it all before. The older O'Malley was asserting his authority. "You did the same." He indicated with his chin towards the extras.

"My prerogative. Step forward."

Nash did as he was told and with the wave of a hand from Colin, one of his men stepped forward and began patting the federal officer down. Straightening up and moving back the man turned to Colin and said, "He's good."

"Now that your boy there has had his thrills by feeling me up, how about we get this thing done?"

"You got the money?"

"In the car."

"Get it and we'll get our package."

Nash frowned wondering what was meant by package instead of product. He turned and walked back to the car, scratching his head as he opened the rear door on the passenger side. As he took the bag of cash from it, he whispered to Gloria, "Muriel."

The detective sergeant stiffened when she heard the name. When Nash was young, he'd had a dog, a Blue Heeler bitch named Muriel. And bitch had been a good word for her because she was always biting him just for the hell of it. Then one day Muriel had gone too far, and Nash's father had taken the dog away and shot it. It was two weeks before Nash spoke to his father afterward. It was Nash's way of telling her something wasn't right.

She said, "Something's wrong. Be ready."

Meanwhile, Nash had walked back to where Colin O'Malley and his brother stood, and dropped the bag on the bitumen at his feet. "Now it's your turn."

The older O'Malley stared over Nash's shoulder and said, "All in good time. First your friend. The bitch in the car."

"What about her?"

"Get her out here where we can see her."

"No. She stays there. She has nothing to do with this."

Colin grew angry and snapped at the federal officer. "You fucking brought her here. She's part of it if I say she is, boyo. Now get her out here."

The two bodyguards with the O'Malleys reached under their coats and left their hands there. No doubt they rested on the butts of their sidearms. *OK, let's play along and see where this takes us.* Nash turned and waved Gloria out of the vehicle.

She climbed out of the Commodore and walked towards the group. "What's up, baby?" she asked, chewing on a pretend piece of gum.

"Just stand there and keep your mouth shut," he ordered her.

"What? Why?" Gloria asked seemingly perplexed.

"Search her," Peter O'Malley ordered, speaking for the first time.

The tough who'd searched Nash moved forward again and reached out to touch Gloria. As he did, she swatted his hand away. "What the fuck?"

He tried again. "Hey! Keep your hands off me, arsehole."

This time however the man wasn't about to be swayed and

pressed in closer. Again, Gloria put on her best bimbo protest. "Hey, back off. Don't touch me. No, leave me alone. *Fuck off!*"

Her last words were more forceful than her previous ones and as she said them, she swung an open palm up and it cracked against the man's left cheek. He staggered back and reached for his personal weapon. Gloria however had turned her head towards Nash and said with a raised voice, "He deserved that. He touched my tit. There's nobody I don't know touches my fucking tits. I ain't no whore."

"Hey," Nash snapped. "Back off. Leave her alone."

The bodyguard glanced at Colin O'Malley searching for guidance. "Leave her," he said. "For now."

The man backed away and Gloria hurried across to stand close to Nash, her left shoulder tucked in behind his right. He felt something behind his back and felt the Glock slide inside, the foresight scraping his skin. He loved her guts, but it was a damned foolish move.

"Now, Mister Trent, where were we?"

"You were about to show me some product."

"Yes, I was, wasn't I?"

He turned back and said to the other bodyguard. "Get it."

Nash and Gloria watched on as the man walked over to the second vehicle. However, when the rear passenger door was opened, it wasn't a bag of drugs brought forth, but a woman.

Alarm bells went off in Nash's head. Now he was certain something was wrong. Two more doors opened, and two men climbed out, turning to roughly manhandle a third man from the rear door. They dragged him forward and thrust him into the light towards where they stood. Now there were seven including the O'Malleys. But this latest guy didn't appear to be too much of a threat.

"Hello, Mister Nash," a woman said with a heavily accented voice.

A cold hand touched Nash's soul as the woman moved into the light. It was Betty O'Malley. She was a hard-looking bitch with numerous lines tracking like roadmaps across her face. And, like her sons, her hair was red. "Shit."

Beside him he felt Gloria stiffen and he reached out with his right hand to steady her. But it was not necessary; as an UC, like him, she'd been in positions like this many times before. Their success rate was high, with the exception of the last time which had ended badly. He'd gone batshit crazy and killed a handful of people. But surely this couldn't get that bad. Could it?

It did. The third person dragged from the Toyota was none other than a bruised and battered Craig French.

"Double shit."

FOUR HOURS EARLIER

Craig French hated stakeouts in the middle of the day. He always figured that whoever was doing it, stood out like the proverbial dogs' balls, and was easily made. His vehicle was parked along the street from Betty O'Malley's four bed brick suburban home. One thing the woman didn't do was flaunt her wealth. And there could be no mistake; the woman was rolling in money.

An old Ford Fairlane chugged along Daisy Street, its V8 engine louder than normal with a hole in its exhaust. It pulled up in a concrete driveway across the street from where he was seated in his gray Ford Falcon, with the darkest legal window tint to make it harder for anyone to see inside.

From the Fairlane climbed a young couple—he assumed they were a couple. Both appeared to be in their late teens, Frenchy figured. The guy was unshaven, his face covered in peach fuzz. His jeans were halfway down his ass and his boxers were showing. The girl had dirty blonde hair and wore tight fitting cutoff shorts that exposed the creamy white flesh of her lower buttocks. She also wore a pink tube top with no bra, the chilly weather making her nipples stand erect like a honeymooner's dick.

She glanced across the street at Frenchy's car and said something to her boyfriend who turned to look in the Falcon's direction. He stared for a handful of seconds and then went to the rear of the car and used the key to open the trunk.

Frenchy stiffened expectantly and rested his hand on his Glock in its holster. But the young man grabbed a carton of VB cans and slung it onto his shoulder before slamming the lid shut. He walked past his girlfriend who stood rooted to the spot, once more casting her gaze at the Falcon. She then lifted her top to expose her breasts and jumped up and down so they bounced vigorously.

"Silly cow," Frenchy muttered as she pulled the top back

into place and followed her boyfriend inside.

The episode just confirmed his suspicions that stakeouts on streets like this were a bad idea. His phone rang and he picked it up. It was Gloria. "Yes, boss?"

"Nash and I are leaving Melbourne for a meet with the O'Malleys. I want you to stay there and keep an eye on Betty. Got it?"

"Yes, ma'am."

"Don't screw it up. If you get caught out this could all turn to shit and I won't be happy. I'll check in with you in half an hour."

"Yes, ma'am," *he repeated.*

"And don't call me ma'am."

"Yes, Sarge."

"Asshole," *she muttered and hung up.*

Frenchy returned his focus to the target house. The street was quiet once more, and for the next ten minutes nothing transpired. He was becoming bored and a little restless when he noticed the young woman from across the street closing the front door to her house.

Without hesitation she walked down her driveway and across the street to the Falcon Frenchy was sitting in.

"Shit," *he growled. This was getting worse.*

She tapped on his window.

"Go away," *he said.*

She tapped some more.

"Go away."

The third time she tapped she didn't stop until he wound the window down. "*What do you want?*" *he asked abruptly.*

"*What are you doing?*" *she asked, curiosity evident in her voice.*

"*Nothing.*"

"*You have to be doing something,*" *she stated, cocking her hip and leaning over to get a better look.* "*You a cop?*"

"*No,*" *Frenchy lied.* "*Who are you?*"

"*Mary.*"

"*OK, Mary, I'm waiting for someone.*"

"*Uh huh. You want a blow job?*"

He studied her for a moment noting the black rings around her eyes and the track marks on her arms. Junkie. "*What?*"

"*You want me to blow you? I won't charge much. Give me twenty bucks and I'll do it.*"

"*No, I don't want you to blow me. What about your boyfriend?*"

Mary smiled showing even white teeth. "*He's in the shower. Don't worry about him, you'll be done by the time he's finished.*"

"*No, I don't want a blow job,*" *Frenchy growled, his gaze unwavering as he stared into her blue eyes.*

She pulled her top down so her breasts were exposed. "*You sure? I'll let you spurt on my titties.*"

"*Damn it, piss off.*"

The sudden rush of air from outside made him jump and Frenchy felt the pressure of a gun muzzle in his side. A voice with an Irish accent said, "*What the fuck do you think you're doing in my street, pig?*"

The girl smiled at Frenchy once more; this time there was

no emotion in it. She said, "See, you should have let me suck your dick. At least you would have died happy."

"I believe that you are all acquainted," Colin O'Malley stated. "Which leaves me with a bit of a dilemma."

Nash and Gloria remained silent.

The older O'Malley continued. "I try to stay clear of killing police officers. It makes things awfully messy for our business. That was the reason we had to leave Ireland you know. A nosey copper poked his beak in where it wasn't wanted. I had to kill him which made things start to heat up. Looks like it's about to happen again, and that really pisses me off."

"I'm sorry," Frenchy blurted out.

"It's OK, Frenchy."

"Isn't that sweet. The young man's sorry. I'm sorry, too," Colin snapped and produced a handgun from inside his coat and shot Frenchy in the head.

Nash could see it coming and he was too late to intervene and prevent it. He watched as the young constable fell to the asphalt at his feet and something inside Nash snapped, much like it had done that time before.

With a roar, Nash ripped the Glock from his waistband and brought it around from behind his back. The smug expression on Colin O'Malley's face turned to horror as he realized that the man before him was armed. He fought to bring his weapon around but was pitifully slow, and the first shot that Nash fired blew Colin's brains out the back of his head.

A loud screech emanated from the lips of Betty O'Malley as she realized that her first born had just been put down like a rabid dog. Nash ignored the woman and concentrated on the second of the O'Malley brothers. Peter's hand wrestled with his coat to pull his own weapon, but Nash's Glock fired twice more, and the bullets punched into Peter's chest. Nash advanced towards the bodyguards and had one of them down before Gloria or the others could react, still stunned by the violence of what had just happened to one of their own.

The bodyguard who'd frisked him and attempted the same on Gloria was the next one to die. Two more bullets to the chest and his night was over.

From out of the darkness came the whiplash of a carbine, and a 5.56 round ended the life of another bodyguard.

That left two more, and both had now sought refuge behind one of the SUVs. Gloria fired three shots at one of them with her own weapon and the sound of bullets punching into the Toyota was audible even over the gunfire. The report of each shot was whipped away on the wind, out across the lake's open expanse.

The remaining bodyguards opened fire and bullets whizzed close to Nash's head. "Get down, you dickhead!" Gloria shouted at him. But he was still too pissed to give any thought to his own safety.

Nash circled to his left to open the angle on one of the shooters. Out of the corner of his eye he saw Gloria move right to do the same thing. Suddenly the former undercover stopped firing as the slide on his weapon locked back. He dropped out the magazine and slapped another home. The slide came forward and he was ready to shoot once more.

Reaching out of the darkness more bullets from Annie and Leroy peppered the Toyota. Sirens grew loud in the distance as the Benalla police responded to the shattering gunfire. A cry of pain emanated from behind the SUV and one of the remaining bodyguards staggered into the open. Nash sighted along his barrel and shot him in the chest.

One left.

The gravity of his situation had a profound effect on the shooter, seeing all the others brought down before his eyes, and he threw his weapon out onto the gravel.

"Don't shoot! I give up."

Nash turned to look for Betty O'Malley and found her crouched over the prostrate form of Colin, crying. He strode over to her and placed the gun against her head. Gloria had seen him like this only once before and she knew what was about to happen. "Nash, stop!"

He glanced around at Gloria, murder in his eyes. "She deserves it," he hissed.

"Not like this. She's lost her sons. Let her think about that as she rots in prison."

Betty looked up at him, her face a mixture of tears and hatred. "Go on, do it. If you don't, I'll come after you and kill you myself. You bastard."

"Let it go, Nash," Gloria said. "She'll pay for what she's done. And God knows her sons have."

Nash hesitated, wanting badly to pull the trigger and put a

bullet in Betty O'Malley's skull. He lowered his gun and then tucked it inside his pants just as the Benalla coppers arrived, red and blue lights dancing through the dark sky.

"Four men! You shot and killed four fucking men! Christ, Nash, I should throw you out of this place right now," Commander Mack McKenzie shouted loud enough to be heard down the hall from his office. "Under normal circumstances you should be put on leave until after the review. But the mountain of paperwork you'll need to fill out will keep you busy until then. Shit a frigging brick."

For a moment, Nash thought his boss was going to come across his desk, instead the man stood up and turned away to look out his window.

McKenzie was a former NSW Policeman from Sydney, but the previous year he'd been tapped, transferred, and placed in charge of Gloria Browning's new taskforce. Codenamed Taskforce Lucifer.

But the shooting was only the tip of the iceberg as far as Mack and Nash went. The animosity between them was far more deep-seated, stemming from the time that Nash had had a one-night stand with the man's wife. Of course, Nash hadn't been aware of her identity at the time, but as far as Mack was concerned, it didn't mean shit.

Mack turned to face Nash, his brown eyes glittering with rage. Although only in his late thirties, his hair was rapidly turning gray. If Nash worked under him for much longer, he'd be white come next Christmas.

"It wasn't his fault, Mack," Gloria said.

"Whose fault was it then, Gloria? Did you shoot four suspects?"

"They weren't suspects," said Nash. "They—"

"Shut up. When I want you to talk, I'll tell you what to say." McKenzie threw his hands in the air before rubbing his face and running them through his hair in frustration.

Gloria knew that Nash was only going to take so much before he snapped and did something he would regret. "Mack, they killed Craig. Just shot him down in cold blood right there in front of us. They were going to kill the rest of us, too."

"You had backup."

"They were too far away. If Nash hadn't reacted the way he did, they would have gunned down at least one of us, if not both."

Mack shifted his steely gaze to Nash. "It would have made my day if it'd been you."

"Fuck you," Nash said in a low voice ripe with menace.

"What?" McKenzie looked almost apoplectic.

"Sorry. Fuck you, sir." The look of contempt on his face was evident.

"Get out of my office before I suspend you right now!" McKenzie thrust one arm at the door, restraining his anger by clenching his other fist on his hip.

"Go right ahead," Nash growled as he turned and walked out, slamming the door behind himself.

Mack glared at Gloria. "I don't know what you see in him,

Gloria. I'm damned if I do."

"He's good at what he does," she responded simply.

"He's a loose cannon," Mack growled. "Now, tell me what you've got."

"It's only just the start but at the moment we've found at least one container of ecstasy pills on the Melbourne docks and the canary that surrendered to us at Nillahcootie tells us that there are at least another two."

"What did I hear about bodies?"

"Apparently, he's ready to cut a deal and tell us where Johnson and Richards are. All he wants is witness protection and a get out of jail free card."

Mack raised his eyebrows. "Johnson and Richards?"

"Yes, sir."

"They've been off the grid for over twelve months."

"More like fourteen."

Once one of the biggest crime bosses in Melbourne, Ted Johnson and his girlfriend Jess Richards had gone missing one night and hadn't been seen or heard from since. The only trace ever found was Johnson's blue Ford Mustang. Burnt out on a secluded road on the Mornington Peninsula.

"He's saying he knows what happened to them?"

"That's what he's alleging."

"All right, get back down to Melbourne, put him in a room and tell him he doesn't get a deal unless he gives us something. Leave tomorrow."

"Sure. I'll get Nash—"

"No, not Nash. You and Leroy." He cut her off and his tone

told her he would brook no argument.

Gloria wasn't happy but wasn't willing to push it just yet because Mack was starting to calm down. "OK. Me and Leroy."

"When you find out something bring it back to me and I'll do what I can."

"Yes, sir."

Nash was sitting in the team's briefing room and appeared to be staring trancelike at the magnetic whiteboard covered in notes. It was actually a photo of Craig French stuck to the noticeboard that he was staring at when Gloria found him.

"Are you OK?" she asked him, looking to see what was so riveting.

"I'm fine. You'd think he'd get over it by now."

"You did screw his wife, Nash," she reminded him blithely.

He smiled. "I did, didn't I. No one's ever going to let me forget that, are they? What about you? I screwed you too, remember?"

"We have the evidence to prove it."

"Mighty fine evidence if you ask me," he said, allowing his thoughts to focus on something positive rather than the what ifs: their daughter.

"Are you coming over tonight?" Gloria asked.

"Maybe."

"Rachel would love to see you."

"What about you?"

She shrugged. "Bring your toothbrush. We'll see what happens. Tomorrow, I have to go to Melbourne and talk to our friend Alonzo."

"Alonzo?"

Alonzo was the name of the remaining bodyguard. "Yes. Mack wants to know a thing or two before he agrees to an immunity plea."

Nash climbed to his feet. "Fine, I'll come with."

"Slow your roll, sunshine. Mack doesn't want you anywhere near this. He thinks you're too volatile."

Gloria thought he was about to explode but he surprised her by nodding instead. "That's fine with me. Got too much shit to write out anyway."

"Tends to happen when you shoot four people."

"He's never going to let me forget it, is he?" Nash asked.

"Probably not."

"That's it then. I'm done. I'm going back to being a private investigator."

"What?" Gloria was stunned. "What do you mean, Dave?"

"You lot are better off without me. Plus, after what happened to Frenchy, I think I've had enough."

"Whoa, slow down a minute, Dave. Take some time, think about it for a few days, even a week. Then make a decision. At least wait until I return from Melbourne."

He stared at her. He owed her at least that much. "All right. But only if I can look after Rachel while you're gone."

She smiled at him. "I can live with that."

OUTBACK
WESTERN AUSTRALIA

Swinging the pick with a grunt, the man swore when the pointed end made little headway in breaking up the rock-hard red crust. He swung again, dislodging a small clump and some little stones, feeling gratified that it was moving, but frustrated at the prospect of the length of time it would take him to finish the job. He swung the wooden handled tool for another minute before stopping for a breather, dropping the pick and picking up the shovel to scrape the loose stuff out of the hole. Alternating use of the tools until it was four feet deep, he then threw the tools aside, wiping his gloved hands across his sweaty brow. The man looked up at the clear blue, cloudless sky, taking several deep breaths to get his wind back. The day was already hot, the temperature rising rapidly as the morning sun crept higher. A large crow circled lazily above him on hot thermals.

"Not today, old crow," the man muttered, pulling himself up out of the hole. He turned and studied his work and then looked at the mound of red dirt he'd cast to one side.

Stretching his back as he walked toward his vehicle, he headed directly to the rear where an old green canvas tarpaulin covered the tray. He reached out to draw it back when it moved. The man hesitated and then grasped a ratty and torn rope hole corner, drawing it to one side.

"Hello," he said with a broad smile, eyes sparkling with anticipation.

Lying naked in the vehicle's tray was a young man, his body a mass of burns, bruises, cuts and abrasions. One part of his upper thigh was crusted thick with dried blood where the skin had been peeled away with a sharp knife. The white skin of his bare chest was also a rusty brown colour. Across his mouth was a short strip of silver duct tape, effectively stifling his pleas. The man pouted playfully, his voice taking on a high-pitched whiney tone as he said, "I'm afraid you're no fun anymore. It seems you can't run." His voice returned to normal, and he grinned at the prospect of what was to come. "Your friend, however, will be enough for a while. Do you think she can last?"

A young woman, no more than nineteen, began to squirm beside the fearful young man. She'd been spared the physical torture her companion had been subjected to. But not the mental. Her eyes were red from crying, her face streaked where the runnels had tracked down her dusty cheeks. Like her friend she was gagged and naked, her athletic body on display.

Hearing the crunch of boots on gravel, the man turned to watch another man approach the vehicle. "Should we leave the gag on her?"

"Yeah. It's no fun otherwise. I'm sick of hearing the women cry and scream. That ruins it for me."

The first man edged around to the rear tailgate. "Might as well get it done before we have our fun."

The naked guy's eyes widened with fear as the man opened the rear of the tray—dropping the tailgate with a clang as it swung and hit the taillights—leaned forward and began dragging him out of the back. The young man kicked and grunted; his screams choked off by the tape. The large scab on his left thigh split and fresh blood oozed from the ghastly wound. Hitting the hard ground with a thump, he yelled behind his gag at the pain, before being dragged across the rough terrain towards the shallow grave. Sharp stones sliced open the skin on his back and he grimaced in pain.

From the rear of the vehicle the young woman's muffled pleas could be heard but were basically ignored by the two men who went about their business.

With a final heave they threw the young man in the hole, then paused. Staring down at the pleading eyes for a long time, they shivered at the delicious exhilaration coursing through their bodies, the power they held in their grasp.

One of them said, "Wait there, I'll be right back."

The man hurried over to his vehicle and opened the passenger door. He reached behind the seat and pulled out a .308 caliber rifle, and a machete—the cutting edge honed razor sharp. He looked at both, shrugged his shoulders, and then put the machete back.

As he walked back to the grave, he worked the bolt on the rifle. Standing above the young man he raised it to his shoulder and fired. Just the one shot. No sense in being inhumane about it.

He looked up at his friend. "Let's do it."

They walked back to their vehicle and looked down at the young woman. One of them smiled lasciviously. "Your turn."

Her tear-filled eyes widened as their hands reached for her. She started to struggle fiercely, kicking out with her feet as they dragged her from the back of the vehicle.

"Take it easy, girly," one of them said. "We're not going to hurt you. Not yet anyway."

They stood her erect, a sorrowful figure against the stark red desert and the clumps of spinifex. Pulling a knife from a sheath at his hip, one of the men walked behind the young woman and grabbed at the ropes binding her wrists. She struggled once more, so he leaned in near her ear and said, "If you don't want me to cut you, then keep still."

She froze in fear, feeling the ropes finally give way and then her hands were free. He reached and removed the gag.

"Hey," the other one protested, "I thought you said we were going to leave the gag on."

"Changed my mind." The guy shrugged, as though it should be obvious that it was his prerogative to do as he pleased.

"D—don't hurt me. P—please," she stammered. She looked from one man to the other, beseeching them with her eyes as well as her words.

"Run," the man said to her.

"W—what?" She looked at him askance.

"Run!" the man shouted into her ear.

The young woman lurched forward suddenly, not needing to be told twice, and started a shuffling lope, the rocks and gravel cutting into her feet. She glanced back over her shoulder, staggered, stumbled, regained her footing and shuffled on."

"Run!" the man shouted again, and her lope grew faster.

The man looked at his friend who said, "How long are we going to give her?"

"Ten minutes. Get me a beer."

The pair stood in the dusty sunshine, drinking their beer and using the condensation on the cans to wipe their sweat-beaded foreheads, all the while watching the young woman grow smaller in the distance across the flat plain. She was tracking towards a large flat-topped hill which stood like a sentinel over the desert. Beyond it were more of the same, topped with stunted trees, their exposed faces scarified by the passage of time.

"They always run that way," the first man said as he swatted at an annoying fly.

The second man nodded, bored with the wait. "Is it time yet?"

"Yeah, get the dogs."

CHAPTER TWO

TWELVE MONTHS LATER

The rotting kangaroo lay in the middle of Dillwarra's main street, ripening by the minute as the outback sun climbed higher into the sky and the temperature passed a lazy forty degrees. Dave Nash strode slowly past it, the sound of the buzzing flies growing loud as the swarm was routed from their rancid repast as his shadow fell across them.

As the rest settled down to resume their feast, one landed on his cheek, its sticky feet crawling over the stubble on his face. Mindful of where it had just been, he swatted it away with his left hand. His right held a Winchester .243 caliber lever-action rifle. Rivulets of moisture rolled down his cheeks. Underneath the sweat-stained Akubra, blue eyes darted nervously left and right as Nash kept slowly walking forward.

The body of Police Sergeant Hank Groves lay back beside the white Landcruiser in a pool of rapidly drying blood. His partner, Senior Constable Tom Price was also down, but continued to cling to life. Nash hoped that he would be able to hold on until help arrived.

Somewhere in this deserted outback town, the killers who Nash had been hunting for the past two weeks were hiding out. The problem was that the police had beaten him to it and as a result, had paid a heavy and unexpected price. Damn it, he'd left the Federal Police Taskforce to get away from this shit.

Nash had been engaged to investigate the disappearance of a young stockman from a west Queensland property. The jackaroo's parents, John and Peta Timmins, who lived in Acacia Ridge, a suburb of Brisbane, had contacted Nash through his office in Emerald.

They'd been trying to reach their son Marcus at Redgum Station but had heard nothing back. Hughes, the owner, had told them that the lad had left a couple of weeks before, and when the police had asked questions and got nothing, it was just assumed that young Timmins had moved on.

That was when Nash had been brought in. He'd been living in Emerald for the past eight months. An Outback PI he called himself. Surprisingly, the work was steady. Nothing flash but it paid the bills.

Mostly of his cases involved missing or stolen farming equipment. Every now and then the suspected affair. However, this was his first missing persons case since quitting the force, and it had all blown up in spectacular fashion.

He'd arrived in a small town where the roads were rough,

and a thick coating of dust settled on every piece of furniture daily as it blew in from the west. It was hot, and throughout summer, afternoon thunderstorms rolled across the dry landscape with monotonous regularity, dropping enough rain to fill puddles, not dams. In places it was called a green drought.

While asking questions in search of answers, Nash had established that Marcus Timmins had fallen in with the wrong crowd; or rather, had gone to work for them.

The station on which he'd been employed had been doing it hard throughout the drought and needed a source of income. What the owner provided was a waystation for stolen cattle being moved north for the livestock ships out of Darwin.

The setup was large scale, including underground water tanks that were filled monthly, paddocks of stock holding yards, and wide gravel turnarounds for fast and easy access for B-double road trains. Weekly cattle shipments were overnighted in the yards before being reloaded the following day to be moved on.

From what Nash had been able to ascertain, there was another station somewhere in the Territory where the animals were unloaded, rebranded, and with new paperwork issued for them, they were then delivered to the port.

In all, it was a multi-million-dollar operation.

However, a spanner had been jammed in the works, threatening to bring down the whole setup; a spanner named Marcus Timmins. Timmins had been brought up in a loving family, and his moral standing was a problem. According to Ingersol, another of the hands, Marcus, Grant, and Thommo had gone out kangaroo shooting to get meat for the station dogs, and they'd returned without him.

Nash was reasonably certain that Ingersol was telling the truth because he could hear the fear in the man's voice when he'd questioned him. But Ingersol had also said that Grant and Thommo were the ones used when there was any sort of problem. They were experts at making issues disappear. One way or the other.

Taking what he knew to the police, Nash was summarily dismissed after they'd listened to him, and said that they'd look into it. "Really? Is that it?" he'd asked the aging Sergeant Groves.

"Son," the tone of the man's voice had been condescending, "son, I already told you, we'd look into it."

"I'm telling you that I have a witness that these blokes took Timmins out and didn't come back with him. I'm also telling you that they did something to him."

"Where is this witness?" The sergeant had a doubtful look on his face.

Nash sighed. "He was scared and shot through."

Tom Price had given a derogatory snort. "Sounds like someone who's got an axe to grind to me."

"And you're a dickhead," Nash had snapped at him in frustration.

Words had been exchanged back and forth and Groves had threatened him with arrest. "I know all about you, hotshot," he'd said. "Damn cowboy who thinks he's all that."

"What?"

"Talked to your former boss. Told us all about how much of a loose cannon you were."

Nash had shaken his head and walked out wondering whether the dry dust had somehow leached into their brains and killed most of the cells that might have lived there at one time.

So, continuing his search for more information had brought him to the ghost town of Dillwarra; a product of the drought. Stations going broke could no longer afford to employ hands; no jobs meant no income or customers for the shops. Without customers the businesses went broke. Little towns just couldn't afford to live and slowly they died like grapes left to wither on a vine.

But unknown to him, Groves and Price had done their own investigating, whether shamed into it by the blow-in, he didn't know, but when he'd arrived, both coppers were down and now he was all alone with three men, Grant, Thommo, and the station owner, Hughes, somewhere in the town, all with no compunction about killing. Nash had compiled a file on the three, including licence photos so he would recognize each of them on sight.

The conclusions Nash had drawn had come from following the money. You see, with a station as far gone as Redgum, one just couldn't pay off lump sums and expect to get away with it. So, Hughes needed a safe place to keep his money. And a large safe it was, too; in a defunct bank in a deserted town.

With gravel crunching beneath his boots, and flies around his head, his eyes were darting from left to right. Further along the main street he found what he was looking for. The battered sign said Dillwarra Country Credit Union. Parked front-end in outside the building was a light brown 4X4.

"That's far enough, Nash," a voice called out. "Just turn around and walk away."

Nash stopped. A fly buzzed past his head, but he made no sudden movements. He knew that as soon as he turned his back, they'd gun him down. His gaze never stopped flicking back and forth. Then he saw the glint of sunlight on glass. His eyes were drawn to the water tower at the far end of the street. Someone was up there with a rifle.

Without hesitating, Nash darted to his left. A shot cracked and a bullet passed through the air where he'd been not two heartbeats before. The bullet ricocheted off the asphalt and screamed into the distance.

Nash ran as fast as he could towards the shopfront opposite him. It had a large glass window and an alcove containing the wood and glass entry door. He didn't take the time to see what the name of the store was. Another shot rang out, the bullet hitting the metal front above the store next door with a clang.

From somewhere along the street, he heard a shout. "Get the bastard, you useless prick!"

But by the time the third round was buzzing through the heat-filled air, Nash was already tucked inside the relative safety of the alcove.

His chest heaved with each gulped breath of the scorching atmosphere. Sweat rolled down his stubbled cheeks and over his neck, the collar of his shirt wet. He spoke quietly to himself, "This could be an issue."

Easing his head around the corner of the alcove, Nash looked back along the street. At first, he saw nothing; the street appeared to be clear. Within moments, he noticed one of the three men he was looking for duck from an alcove, much like the one he was using, and move to the next.

Backing up against the door of the store, Nash contemplated his options and next move. He reached out and tried the handle, but it was locked. Grunting in disgust, he wondered what the point was of locking a door in a deserted town? It wasn't like someone was going to steal anything. He raised a boot and kicked it. The door crashed back, and he entered the room.

It was hard to tell what the shop had once been, now just an empty dust-covered space with bare shelves and an empty glass counter.

Nash hurried through the desolate space towards the rear door. He shook his head in amusement as, once again, he found the door locked. Turning the latch, it snicked free of the receiver, and he pulled the door open, discovering that it led out to a concrete driveway which appeared to service the shop he was in as well as those to either side.

Stepping out of the door he looked off to his left. From where he stood, the water tower was clearly visible which meant they could possibly see him. He stepped back quickly and brought the butt of the rifle up to his shoulder, taking a deep breath and expelling it before lifting the barrel.

Then once more he edged out into the open, sweeping the

rifle around until his sights settled on the water tower. For a few agonising seconds he looked for his target, hoping he would see him before the sniper could shoot.

"Come on, where are you?" Nash muttered, growling quietly until he found him. The shooter was hidden in the deep shadow cast by the water tower, but he was up there.

Nash squeezed the trigger and the Winchester slammed back into his shoulder. There was no cry of pain following close on the heels of the rifle's report. Nor was there any display of the shooter throwing his arms in the air like they did in the movies. The man simply slumped forward, losing his grip on his rifle, and it fell towards the ground.

Levering a round into the breech, Nash glanced behind him in time to see the man who'd been working his way along the street come through the open shopfront door. It was Grant, and by a process of elimination, that meant that the shooter on the water tower had to have been Thommo.

Grant panicked at the sight of Nash and fired from the hip. The bullet flew wide and punched through the thin wood wall to Nash's left at head height. Nash responded while Grant fumbled with the bolt of his rifle. The Winchester crashed and the .243 round hammered into Grant's middle doubling him over.

The killer slumped to his knees, releasing the rifle as he clutched at his stomach. He looked up at Nash, his face red, his lips quivering. "You prick, you gut shot me."

"Don't go anywhere."

"Fuck you."

Nash walked over to him, the Winchester unwavering in his hands. He bent down and picked up the rifle Grant had dropped and took a step back. He removed the bolt and tossed it and the rifle aside. "Where is he, Grant?"

"Who?"

"Who do you think?"

The wounded killer groaned. "Get stuffed, Nash."

"Is he at the bank?"

"G—go and find out for y—yourself, bastard."

"Oh, don't worry, I plan to."

"Watch out for Thommo," Grant said with a weak smile. "He's better with a gun than I ever was."

"No, he's not. He's dead."

A string of pained epithets followed him out the door.

Nash started along the footpath towards the old credit union. A crow cawed from the top of a building across the street as it watched his progress. There was a noise behind him, and Nash swung around to see a dog, a Blue Heeler nosing around the two policemen on the street, one dead, the other probably not far from it.

"Shit," he growled and then turned back to face the direction he was headed. His heart beat at a rapid rate; his breathing grew louder in his ears as he strained to hear anything that might give away Hughes's position. Then he saw it. Just a flicker of movement in the shadows of the old bank which warned him to move.

A rifle whiplashed, the PI rolled to his left before coming up onto his knees, the high-powered round fizzing through the air where Nash had just been. He brought the rifle up to his shoulder, sighted where the shot came from and fired, not expecting Hughes to have remained in the same place after shooting his weapon.

It was a howl of agony and dismay that rolled along the street, an animal-like sound which told Nash that his bullet had found its mark.

Nash came to his feet and walked slowly towards the bank.

Hughes was dead. His body lay under the awning out the front of the credit union. The bullet had ripped through his chest, destroying everything it touched. The man's eyes were open and staring sightlessly at Nash who stood over him.

The PI reached into his pocket for his phone. He pressed a button, surprised to see that he had signal. He placed it to his ear and waited for an answer.

CHAPTER THREE

**EMERALD
QUEENSLAND**

"Are you alright?" Gloria asked him.

Nash nodded. "Anything happen while I was away?"

"Don't avoid the question, Dave," Gloria said.

A high-pitched squeal interrupted where the conversation was headed, and Rachel appeared. "Daddy's home."

She barreled into his arms, and he scooped her up. Her blue eyes sparkled, and her smile widened. "What did you bring me?"

Her held her close and could smell the fresh apples smell of the shampoo they all used, in her long dark hair. "Nothing this time, sweetie."

For a moment she seemed disappointed before her smile came back and she wrapped her arms tighter around his neck. "Love you, Daddy."

"Love you, too, munchkin."

He looked at Gloria who frowned at him for using their daughter to deflect the conversation she wanted to have.

They had made the move north to Queensland after a long discussion following her return from Melbourne. Deciding to give it another shot, they'd chosen Emerald as the location, mainly because Gloria had a sister there.

Finding a rental house hadn't been too hard and after they'd unpacked and settled in, Nash had set about getting his business up and running, while Gloria had wasted no time in finding employment. He looked at her Queensland Police uniform. Strings had been pulled and she'd been offered a probationary role in Emerald. It was like a fall from grace, having to start at the rank of constable.

Nash saw her still waiting impatiently. He kissed Rachel and put her down. "You'd better go and watch some TV, munchkin, while I talk to Mummy."

"All right."

She skipped away into the living room, content in the fact that her family was together, and they heard the television go on. Gloria said, "I've seen a report of what happened, Dave. I know what happened officially."

"How—"

"Former Federal copper, remember? I have ways. Plus, it was all over the news. Christ, two officers killed. Shot down. Not to mention three civilians. Now, spill."

He sat down at the table and told her about the case. She knew most of it anyway through police channels but didn't have the minutiae that Nash alone was privy to. When he was finished, Gloria asked, "Did they find the kid's body?"

He shook his head, looking down and picking at his thumbnail. "Not yet."

"They're calling you a hero, you know?"

He looked up sharply. "Who is?"

"Half the Queensland Police force."

Nash shrugged his shoulders. "I won't say that they got what they deserved, but they got what they deserved."

"I thought you being a private investigator meant our lives were going to be different," Gloria said.

Defensively, Nash jumped to his feet, running his hand through his hair with frustration. "I didn't plan for this to happen, Gloria. When I arrived in that place the coppers were already dead or close to it. I told them what the problem was, and they ignored me. Well at least I thought they did anyway. Apparently, they didn't, but the threat wasn't taken as seriously as it should have been, and these guys treated as dangerous either. If they had, they would still be alive."

Looking up at him, Gloria spoke placatingly, "I didn't say you planned it, Dave."

Nash groaned and let out a sigh, sinking back into the chair. "I'm sorry, Gloria. I'm tired."

"You'll be right to keep an eye on Rachel?"

"Never too tired for that," he assured her.

Gloria nodded and moved towards him. "I'm happy you're home, Dave. Really."

She wrapped her arms around him and kissed his lips.

When she pulled back, she said, "Don't go to sleep on our little girl. She's been asking for days when you're getting home. She wants some dad time."

"Even if I wanted to, I doubt I could," he said with a grin. "I've missed you."

"I'll see you when I get home." She gave him another quick peck on the lips, and he swatted her butt as she pulled away, grabbing her handbag and heading for the door.

"Stay safe."

"Always do."

The phone in his pocket sounded the opening strains of Bohemian Rhapsody and he reached for it before hitting answer. "Nash."

"Dave, it's Amy."

"Amy? Uh, wow, it's been a while."

"Yes. I know. Listen, Danny doesn't know I'm calling you. We need your help."

Nash was right when he said it'd been a while. He hadn't talked to his brother Danny in over two years. They'd never been especially close even as youngsters, but after Nash had become involved in the world of violence he'd created for himself, the gulf between them had widened exponentially into a chasm. That and the fact his family lived in Adelaide. "What is it, Amy?"

"It's Tiffany."

Nash's skin pricked at the mention of his niece. At nineteen, Tiffany was so much older than Rachel, highlighting the substantial age difference between Nash and his older brother.

"Is she in trouble?"

"I—we don't know. She's disappeared."

"How long's it been?"

"Two weeks."

A wave of dread washed over Nash. Tiffany was family and the fact that he was only hearing the news now rankled him. He felt like asking her why the hell it had taken so long to get in contact with him, but instead he remained calm, took a breath and said, "Tell me about it, Amy."

"Tiffany and her boyfriend were traveling through Western Australia a couple of weeks ago when they disappeared. The WA police don't even have any leads. They just seem to have vanished—"

"How were they traveling, Amy?" he asked.

"Dave, you have to understand—"

"Amy?"

"She's like her father. She's headstrong and—"

"How, Amy?" he asked more forcefully.

"They were hitching."

Fuck me! Hitching in this day and age was just asking for trouble. It was bad at the best of times, but Nash was almost certain there were more serial killers out there preying on random people hitching rides, other than the infamous Reg Dunlevy who'd picked up many foreign hitchers in the late eighties and left their bodies in culverts under National Highway One between Cairns and Melbourne. Fifteen that the authorities knew about but homicide detectives on the task force that eventually caught the concreter from Newcastle were reasonably sure he was responsible for at least another five. Nash tried to keep the anger out of his voice. "What on earth were they thinking, Amy?"

"I know," she said, her voice cracking. "But you can't tell young people anything these days."

"You should have come to me earlier, Amy."

"I wanted to," she said weakly. "Danny just—" her voice trailed away.

"Yeah, I understand. Tell me what you know."

She cleared her throat before starting to relate everything she knew. "Tiffany and Rory left Adelaide four weeks ago. They tripped across the Nullarbor until reaching Perth. They stayed there for a week and then they were leaving to head up to Darwin. She rang me the day before they left and said she would call once they reached Port Headland. But she never called."

"Who is Rory?" he asked.

"Rory Williams, her boyfriend."

"How well do you know him?"

"Well enough. They've been together for two years, Dave. He's a good boy. He'd not do anything to Tiffany if that's what you're thinking. We've been through all of this with the Western Australia police."

"I'm just trying to catch up on everything, Amy. I won't know what to think until I ask all the questions, and even then, I can't rule anything out."

"I'm sorry, Dave, but it's just so frustrating."

Nash's voice softened. "I know, Amy. Which way were they going?"

"The Great Northern Highway."

"Is that what Tiffany told you?"

Amy confirmed it with an abrupt, "Yes."

"There's no way she would have gone another way?"

"No. If she said they were going that way then that's the way they went."

Nash knew from experience that kids often told their parents what they wanted them to hear. "And the WA police have turned up nothing?"

"No. They've just listed them as missing," Amy said, desperation in her voice. "What are we going to do, Dave? What if something has happened? What if—"

"Take it easy, Amy. Stay positive. I'll see you sometime in the next few days."

"You're coming here?"

"Yes."

"No, Dave. If Danny—"

He cut her off again. "If you want my help, Amy, then Danny needs to know and will just have to suck it up. Tiffany is family. Besides, I have a daughter of my own and I don't know what I'd do if I were in your shoes. I'm coming and that's it. I'll let you know when I land."

"All right," she replied hesitantly. "I—I'll see you when you get here. Goodbye, Dave."

"Take care, Amy."

Nash scribbled some more notes down on the paper beside him and looked back at the file. Gloria padded softly up behind him and wrapped her arms around him. She leaned forward and kissed the top of his head. "You ready for bed?"

"Yeah," he said.

Gloria frowned. "That wasn't too convincing. What's wrong?"

"I rang WA police earlier this afternoon and asked a few questions about the case. They have nothing. Either no one saw anything, or the investigators are lazy bastards who don't give a shit. I'm going to have a meeting with one of them when I get over there. Now I don't want to believe that, so I did a little digging of my own."

Gloria moved around the table and sat opposite Nash. "You look like you've found something."

"I goggled—"

"Googled," Gloria corrected him with a small smile.

Nash frowned. "What?"

"It's Googled."

"Fine. I Googled Great Northern Highway to find out all I could about it before I headed up there. You know what the top result was?"

"What?"

"A newspaper article titled "The Highway of No Return". You know why?"

"OK. I'll bite. Why?"

"Because over the past ten years fifteen backpackers have disappeared without a trace on that stretch of road. One for each year with a few extras for good measure."

"Is this going where I think it is?" Gloria asked, giving him a curious look.

He passed over a list of names and dates. "You tell me."

She frowned as she read the sheet of paper. "You're missing twenty-eleven, twenty-twelve, and twenty-sixteen."

"Uh huh. What that tells me is that there was no one reported missing in those years."

"If there was something to it, then the WA police would have made a thorough investigation with it," Gloria told him dismissively.

"I know someone did."

"What, the reporter?"

"Yes. Also—" he handed her another piece of paper, "three of those who went missing were found. All were murdered. No one was ever charged because the investigation went nowhere. By the looks of it they were early victims."

"And you found that on the internet?"

"No, the police database."

Gloria read the second sheet of paper and looked up at Nash. "You need to stay out of there. I should report you for stealing my password. Besides, none of these have anything in common. One was shot, another blunt force trauma, the other strangled."

"Yes, they do. They were all found around The Great Northern Highway. All were young women except for one young man who was traveling with the third victim to be found. Of the three who were found, two had been sexually assaulted. All had bite marks, presumably from a wild dog."

"That doesn't mean they were murdered by the same person."

"Come on, Gloria. Look at the dates. Serial killers evolve. Just because the first one was different to the later one doesn't mean it was a different killer."

"If so, then what happened to all of the other bodies?"

"It's a big country out there," Nash replied.

"Dave, I think you're reading too much into this," she said with a shake of her head.

"I guess I'll find out, won't I. I'm going to arrange a meet with that reporter in WA. We'll see what they have to say."

"Fine, you do what you have to do. I'll support you all the way. But for now, come to bed."

Nash nodded. "All right."

CHAPTER FOUR

**ADELAIDE
SOUTH AUSTRALIA**

Unsure whether he was ready for what he was about to do, Nash rapped his knuckles on the door to the brick home and waited for it to be answered. The door swung open, and his brother stood there for a moment before he realized who it was. "Piss off, Dave," he growled, closing the door in Nash's face.

"Come on, Danny, open the door."

"Go away. What are you doing here?"

There were some muted tones from behind the door and then it opened once more. Amy stood there, her face deeply lined with worry, her hair semi-gray. "I'm sorry for that, Dave. Please come in."

Nash picked up his overnight bag and left it in the entrance. Then he followed Amy through to the living room. It was sparsely furnished but the mantel was adorned with pictures of Tiffany. His brother was now seated in a La-Z-Boy recliner. "What are you doing here, Dave?" The look on Danny's face full of scorn as he asked his question again.

"He's here to help, Danny," his wife said, moving and placing a hand on her husband's shoulder.

Dave looked at his brother. The older he got the more he looked like their old man. Right down to the cleft chin.

"Help with what? How does he even know?" Danny asked as he looked up into his wife's worried face.

"Because I called him and asked for his help, Danny. That's why." She stepped back and crossed her arms in defiance.

"Then he can frig off to where he came from. The last thing we need is for his shit to arrive on our doorstep."

"Danny—" Nash started but was cut off.

"I saw what happened on the news, Dave," his brother sneered. "Not happy unless you're shooting someone, huh?"

"That's not fair. You weren't even there. You don't know anything about what happened, Danny."

"Bullshit. You shot four men."

Dave realised he was talking about the events at Nillahcootie.

"Criminals, Danny. They'd just shot a cop and were about to shoot Gloria and me."

"And that makes it all right? I'm sure glad mum and dad aren't still alive to see what a great son you turned out to be."

"Danny!" Amy exclaimed, looking down at him as though she were ashamed of his response.

"Are we going to do this again?" Nash asked his brother. "I came here to help find your daughter. If you don't want it, I'll just head on back to Emerald. I have a family who want and appreciate me there."

Nash turned to leave but Amy stopped him. "Dave, wait."

"I'm wasting my time, Amy."

"No, you're damned well not," she cursed before whirling on her husband. "Listen to me, you stubborn bastard. Dave is here to help us whether you like it or not. And you'd better pissing like it because he's the only chance of you finding your daughter alive."

"If she's alive," Danny muttered. They'd both been thinking it, but this was the first time that either of them had voiced it.

"She is still alive. I know it. We just have to keep believing. Dave, would you like a coffee?"

Nash nodded. "That would be great, thanks, Amy."

"Take a seat and I'll be right back."

Nash sat down and looked at his brother. "She's delusional, you know," Danny said.

"She's holding onto hope, Danny. There's nothing wrong with that, especially when it's all she's got."

He grunted. "A lot of good that will do."

"Tell me what the WA police said," Dave said, trying to move the topic onto the missing couple.

"You're really going ahead with this thing?"

Nash nodded. "Yes. I came all this way, didn't I?"

Danny sighed. "They looked for them and came up empty. Damned cops seemed more concerned that they were hitching than the fact that they'd disappeared. To start with, they checked in with us every day. That was for the first week only. Then they stopped. When I rang to find out what was going on, they said that we would be notified if anything came up."

"Do you have pictures of them? Recent ones?"

Amy appeared and placed the drinks on the coffee table. "I will find them for you. We've something somewhere. We gave the police some already."

She disappeared and Nash said to his brother, "I'm headed to Perth tomorrow. I'll get a vehicle and go north from there. But I have an appointment to meet with a reporter before I leave Perth."

Danny frowned. "What reporter?"

Nash hesitated for a moment then said, "It might be nothing, but she did a piece a while back about the Great Northern Highway."

"What kind of piece?"

"It appears that there have been a lot of people—backpackers, hitchers—disappear in the past along that road. I want to see what her take is on it."

"You mean that there could be a killer operating along the highway?"

Nash nodded. "Not a word to Amy, Danny. Keep it to yourself. I could be barking up the wrong tree. But I promise you this much. If Tiffany is out there, I'll find her."

PORT MELBOURNE WOMEN'S CORRECTIONAL FACILITY VICTORIA

Betty O'Malley sat down across the stainless-steel table from her lawyer, a look of determination on her haggard face. "Do you have it?"

Scott Ballard nodded. He slid the envelope across the table

and Betty opened it. At first glance it seemed to be just legal documents for her to go over. But towards the bottom were the things she really wanted to see. She took out the pictures and studied them while her lawyer spoke. "His name is Dave Nash. He was a federal copper. An undercover operative, but not anymore. He's working as a PI in the middle of nowhere."

"I know that. I saw it on the fecking news channel," she hissed. "He's the one who killed my boys. I want him dead."

"I looked into him, and it seems he's flown the coop, so to speak. He got a phone call, so I was told and is headed to Western Australia. Stopping off in Adelaide along the way."

"What for?"

"Apparently his niece has gone missing."

Betty's eyes lit up. "He has family?"

Ballard nodded. "A brother in Adelaide. Woman and kid in Emerald."

"Does he now?"

"Yes."

"Send Joe Black."

Ballard hesitated a moment. "To do what?"

"To kill them, of course, you blithering fool. Christ, do I have to fecking spell it out?"

"Which ones?"

"Adelaide."

Ballard was a little relieved not to have to have the death of a child on his conscience. "Are you sure?"

"Damn right I am. An eye for an eye. And when he's done that, have him find Nash and do him, too."

"It might be a hard task finding him," the lawyer pointed out.

"If anyone can, Joe Black can. Offer him five-hundred thousand."

"All right, I'll call him as soon as I leave here."

"Make sure you do."

Ballard scooped up the pictures. "Will there be anything else?"

"That will do for a start."

MELBOURNE
VICTORIA

The buzzing of his phone had Joe Black reaching to retrieve it from his left trouser pocket, opening the case and looking at the screen, deciding whether he would take the call. He pressed the green phone. "Yes?"

"My employer has a couple of jobs for you to do. I'll email you the details."

"My usual fee?" Black asked.

"No. This time she will pay five-hundred thousand each job."

"I'm impressed," Black said.

"Give me an hour or so and I'll have everything you need."

"Done."

The line went dead, and Joe Black dropped the phone back in his pocket. Five hundred this time out was a princely sum for his services. But to have it for two jobs was something else.

Joe Black was an ex-soldier who'd served with the ADF or Australian Defence Force. He'd seen action in both Iraq and Afghanistan, after which he'd been honorably discharged and gone to work in the private sector where the money was more encouraging.

While serving as a bodyguard for a rich American oil exec in Iraq, a billion-dollar deal appeared to be about to fall through. While drinking one evening, the exec had said to Black, "I'll pay you one hundred thousand to kill that son of a bitch."

At first, Black thought his boss was joking but after a few tense moments he realized that the man was serious. Black had killed before. Hell, he'd been a soldier. But there was a very real difference between killing for your country and what the man was suggesting. There was no coming back from becoming an assassin. He vacillated briefly before giving his answer. Black's decision sent him down a path of no return.

Putting his military skills to use to set everything up, two days later the target was dead. Problem solved. That had been some years ago now, and he'd not suffered from a guilty conscience once.

An hour later, the alarm for the encrypted email dinged and Black checked the computer. He downloaded the file and printed it off before deleting it.

His target was someone called Nash. A former cop turned private investigator. Also, a couple in Adelaide. The surnames were the same, the investigator's brother. He read through the details supplied and mentally envisioned how he would do it. The first target would be easy enough. Finding Nash would be a little more difficult. Not impossible; just required more work on his behalf.

Black heard the key in the front door lock. He quickly scooped up the papers and put them in a folder he'd put aside for them. Then he put them in his desk.

"I'm home," a voice called from the hallway.

"In my office," he called back.

He could hear the tap of heels on the polished floorboards as his wife traversed their hallway. She entered the office and stopped in front of his desk, looking down at him expectantly. Tori Black was a professional woman. She ran one of the richest investment firms in Melbourne, had dragged it up from the depths to what it was today.

An attractive woman in her late thirties, she wore her long dark hair in a professional upswept style, and her clothes always hugged her athletic form. She smiled at Black, an even-toothed grin which told him that she'd had a good day. "How much?" he asked.

"Ten million, of which I get ten percent."

He nodded. "Nice."

"How was your day?" she asked.

"I have to go away tomorrow," he replied softly as though he was reluctant to do so.

"How long for?"

"A week, maybe."

"A whole week?" she asked mischievously as she started to undo the buttons of her blue silk blouse.

"Uh huh," he nodded.

The blouse dropped to the floor, a lacy black bra holding large firm breasts. It was amazing how a bit of cosmetic surgery could accentuate an already gorgeous body. His eyes drifted down to the six-pack below them, the product of countless hours in their home gym.

Next to go was the pencil skirt, a black lacy thong that matched the bra showed off a taut butt and tanned thighs. Black felt himself stir as he stared at her semi-naked form. He loved it when she made good money.

Still in her heels, Tori walked seductively around the desk and stared at her husband. "A whole week away talking to customers; how am I going to live without you for that long?"

He shrugged. "Heavy machinery is what I do."

"It's a good thing that it pays so well," she replied as the bra was unclipped and fell to the floor.

He nodded as he took in her 'perfect' breasts. "Yes, it is, baby."

ADELAIDE
SOUTH AUSTRALIA

Nash studied the picture of his niece. She was pretty, like her mother. Still, he could see the stubborn streak in her, just by looking at her eyes. That came from her father. And her grandfather.

Nash's old man was the epitome of an ornery old cuss. He could remember an instance of his parents arguing. The pigheaded old thing had not spoken to her for the next two weeks.

"She looks like Amy," Danny's voice cut in.

Nash looked at his brother and nodded. "All except the

eyes."

"Yeah, they're Frank all over."

"Not just Frank," Nash pointed out.

Danny chuckled. "Yeah. Remember the time the old bugger never talked to mum for those two weeks?"

Nash nodded. "All because he thought he was right about something and wouldn't admit he was wrong."

Danny sighed. "I wish I could see those eyes now, Dave."

"You will, Danny," Nash said, knowing that wasn't the case. The girl had been missing for over two weeks. Chances of finding her now, it would be in a shallow grave or in a culvert under some lonely stretch of road.

"How do you expect to find her if the police can't?" Danny asked his brother.

"I have something they don't, Danny. A reason. These guys can only do so much because they often have more than one case on the go. Me, I can focus my full attention on it."

"I hope you find her, Dave. One way or the other for Amy's sake."

"Me, too, Danny. Me, too."

CHAPTER FIVE

PERTH
WESTERN AUSTRALIA

Nash flew out of Adelaide the following day, touching down in Perth almost two hours later. He collected his bag and walked to the car rental desk where he hired a dark blue Commodore for the duration of his stay.

He then drove to a hotel just off Melville Parade where he'd made a reservation prior to leaving Emerald. The suite was tidy, and the double bedroom had a view overlooking the Swan River. There was also a pool and a large dining area as well.

Nash put his bag on the bed and took out his phone. He punched in a number and a familiar voice said, "Mummy's phone."

Nash smiled. "Hey, munchkin, what are you doing answering mummy's phone?"

"Daddy!" Rachel exclaimed excitedly. "When are you coming home?"

"Not for a few days, baby girl."

"Oh."

He could hear the disappointment in her voice, and he wondered if her bottom lip was sticking out the way it usually did when she was crestfallen. "Is mummy there?"

"She's in the toilet," Rachel whispered as though it was a secret. "I think she's—"

"Rachel, what are you doing with my phone?" Nash heard Gloria ask.

"It's daddy, mummy."

"Is it now? What have I said about answering my phone?"

"But it's daddy."

"Rachel."

"I have to go, daddy, she's cross." The softness of her voice made Nash wish he was back home.

"Hi, Dave."

"How are my girls?" Nash asked.

"She is so much like you it isn't funny. I just know that by the time she hits her teenage years she'll have placed half the town under citizen's arrest for some reason or another."

"She gets that from you," Nash told her.

"I don't think so, Dave. How are things?"

"I've not long arrived in Perth. I'm going to see if I can meet with the reporter today instead of tomorrow," he explained.

"How were Amy and Danny?"

Nash sighed. "About as you'd expect. She's hopeful while he

just wants closure for Amy one way or the other."

"I can imagine. I don't know what I'd do if it was Rachel in that situation."

"I do," said Nash. "You'd turn the country upside down until you found her. And that's what I intend to do."

"Yes, you're right."

"Anyway, I'd better go. I'll talk to you later, babe."

"I miss you, Dave."

"I miss you, too. Give our little girl a big kiss, for me."

"Nothing ours about her, asshole," Gloria reminded him. "She's all yours."

"I'm sure you're in there somewhere."

"Good luck finding me."

"Love you."

"Love you, too."

Nash disconnected the call and then looked up the number for the Perth Daily Herald. He dialed the number and a woman picked up on the other end. "Perth Daily Herald, this is Donna, how may I direct your call?"

"Donna, my name is Dave Nash. I was wondering if you could put me through to Maria Gallagher?"

"Wait one moment, sir. Putting you through now."

"Thank you."

There was a buzzing followed by some tinny classical music. After a few more heartbeats, "Maria speaking."

"Maria, Dave Nash. I was wondering if I could meet with you to ask a few questions?"

"Who, sorry?"

"Dave Nash. I'm a private investigator from Queensland."

There was a moment of silence followed by, "Are you the Dave Nash that was involved in that thing a while back?"

"Which thing are you referring to?" Nash asked, cringing with his hand on his forehead.

"Place called Dillwarra."

"You're goggling me, aren't you?"

"It's Google and yes, I am."

"All right, guilty," Nash said with a sigh.

"What can I do for you, Mister Nash?"

"It's Dave and as I said before, I'd like to meet up with you. You pick the place. Preferably today."

"Sounds urgent," she said.

"Could be a life and death matter."

"Now you've really got my interest. Where are you staying?"

He told her.

"There's a pub down the street about five-hundred meters. Meet you there in an hour."

"I'll be there. Thanks."

The pub was called Barney's. It was a decent size with the public bar area reasonably busy with regulars lining the long bar. Nash was at a table in the lounge bar, drinking a beer when Maria Gallagher found him. She was around his height and her eyes were brown and warm, and the tan on her face told of a life outdoors chasing stories for most of her working career.

"Dave Nash?"

Nash nodded and held out his hand. "That'd be me."

"Pleased to meet you." She nodded to his almost empty glass. "Beer?"

"Swan Draught. My shout."

Nash ordered the beer and when it came, Maria picked up hers and said, "Follow me."

He grabbed for his and collected his change, then began to follow her between numerous tables, through a closed door, and into a dining area. She took him to a back corner where they sat at a small table. "So, Mister Nash—"

"Call me Dave."

"So—Dave, what can I do for you?"

"I wanted to ask you about a report you did on the Great Northern Highway a while back if that's all right?"

She frowned, her eyebrows pinching together. "Sure. Is there a reason?"

"My niece and her boyfriend have gone missing up there somewhere and I'm trying to find them."

"Oh, I see. I hope you have some luck."

"Thanks."

"What do you want to know?"

The door to the dining room opened and a man entered, giving them a cursory glance before continuing on his way. Nash waited and then said, "Whatever you can tell me."

Maria expelled a long breath as though just the thought of it was overwhelming for her. "Wow, where to start?"

"What led you to write it?" Nash asked, curious about the events that made her investigate.

"A few years back, the body of a murdered girl was found off the side of the road just north of Mount Magnet. Her name was Grace Townsend. I was sent up there to ask around, get some facts. She was nineteen, had blonde hair, one-seventy centimeters tall. She had no clothes, had been raped, and had bite marks on her body from a dog."

"She was the third one to be found, right?" Nash asked.

Maria took a sip of her beer and nodded. "Yes. I remembered the other two and that's what drove me to look into it further. The other two were Mary Allen and Peggy Lester."

"They were all killed differently, weren't they?" Nash probed, looking for an opinion.

"Yes. Peggy sustained a blunt force trauma from something. Mary was shot, and Grace was strangled."

"Normally that would suggest three different killers," Nash pointed out.

"Killers evolve," she shot back at him.

"Exactly what I said," he muttered.

"What was that?"

"Why do you think it's changed?" Nash asked her.

"You were a cop, you must have a theory," Maria said.

"Only one I can think of," he replied.

"Which is?"

"Tell me the dates the girls were found. The year and month will do."

Maria paused for a moment and said, "Mary was found in Twenty-Ten, March. She was the one who was shot. Peggy Lester in October Twenty-Fifteen. Bludgeoned to death. Grace Townsend was the most recent to be found, August Twenty-Nineteen. She was strangled."

"Did they all have bites?" Nash asked.

"Grace and Peggy did, I'm not sure about Mary."

"So the bites are the only thing linking them?"

"Yes. What are you thinking?"

"That the killer started out by shooting his victims and when that wasn't enough, he got up close and personal. Culminating in the rape and strangulation of Grace Townsend."

"You mean when the buzz wasn't enough anymore the killer changed it up?"

"Something like that," Nash allowed. "Were the victims tested for dog saliva?"

"I couldn't tell you."

"That's all right, I'm meeting with a detective tomorrow. I'll ask him."

"Are you talking about Bruce Morrow?"

"That's the guy."

"Good luck with that." She snorted with derision.

"Why?"

"You'll see," came the cryptic reply.

Nash drank some more of his beer and asked, "What about the gaps in the timeline?"

"Just because there are gaps doesn't mean there weren't any more. Maybe there were some that weren't reported."

Nash nodded. "It wouldn't be the first time." He took out a map. "Could you mark on this where the bodies were found?"

Maria took out a pen and put three crosses on the map. She hesitated and then added another further north near Newman.

"What's that one?" Nash asked.

"Molly Wallace. An aboriginal girl killed in Twenty-Sixteen. She ran out onto the highway and was hit by a truck. The driver couldn't stop. He said it looked as though she was running away from something. He said it was possibly a wild dog."

Nash frowned. "Why wasn't she included?"

"Because all the girls—and boy—who went missing, did so between Paynes Find and the Glengallen Roadhouse north of Meekatharra. Where did your niece go missing?"

"I'm not sure." He paused, thinking. "When you investigated the disappearances, what was the time from them vanishing to being found?"

"It varied. One thing was certain, according to the coroner's report they were all kept alive for a time before they were killed."

"The killer played with them?"

"Yes."

Nash nodded thoughtfully.

Maria finished her beer. "If you've got no more questions, I wish you luck, Nash." She stood and pushed her chair in.

"Thanks for your time." He looked thoughtfully into the bottom of his glass then tipped it up and finished the last mouthful, placing it back on the beer coaster.

Back at the hotel, Nash unfolded the map and studied the four crosses marked by Maria. Three on the highway, one off to the east near a small town. He looked closer at it and marked off the possible towns and roadhouses that Tiffany and her boyfriend might have stopped at.

Roadhouses were good places for hitchers to pick up rides. Kind of like a bus station without having to pay for a ticket. Although, some paid in other ways, including with their lives.

Nash's mobile rang. He picked it up and said, "Nash."

"Mister Nash, it's Bruce Morrow. I'm the detective that's supposed to be meeting with you tomorrow."

Nash closed his eyes and waited for the hammer to fall. 'Supposed to be' always indicated there was bad news to follow. Morrow continued. "Something has come up and I was wondering if tonight might be a convenient time for us to meet?"

"I'll take it," Nash replied quickly.

"There's a pizza place in the city. Mama's. I'll meet you there around seven."

"I'll be there. Thanks."

Joe Black sat across the street from the Adelaide address which he knew to be occupied by Danny and Amy Nash.

He opened the glove compartment and took out his personal weapon and a small case not much bigger than a manicure set. Climbing from his vehicle, he walked across the street and approached the house confidently as though he were expected.

Black rang the doorbell and was greeted by Amy Nash. "Yes? Can I help you."

Black took an ID wallet from his coat pocket and flipped it open. "Sorry to bother you, Mrs. Nash. My name is Brown, I'm a federal police officer from Melbourne. Might I come in, please?"

She hesitated. "What is this about?"

"It's about your daughter."

The two magic words. Your daughter. The door swung wide, and Amy stepped aside. "Please, come in. What was your name again? Can I get you a cup of coffee?"

PERTH
WESTERN AUSTRALIA

Morrow was a thin man with a rundown aura about him, from the rumpled suit and loose knotted tie to his tired eyes. Nash picked him to be in his late forties and found himself wondering if that was a good thing or not. Yes, he had experience, but he might be jaded and cynical, possibly lacking the drive that a younger detective might have. Then again, Nash thought he could be wrong. Time would tell.

The handshake was firm and dry. "Dave Nash."

"Vic Morrow. Well, it's actually Bruce as you know but I get called Vic all the time because of the actor. I respond to both. Are you hungry?"

Nash nodded. "Sure, why not?"

They ordered and made their way back to a corner booth, wanting to be out of the way so no one could hear them talk. Without preamble, Morrow opened with, "I did some checking on you, Nash."

"The media tend to embellish things," Nash said to him, a bit self-consciously.

"Police reports don't."

The private investigator shrugged. "You were looking into

the disappearance of my niece?"

"I was liaising with the other detectives who were."

"What can you tell me?"

"Your niece and her boyfriend were traced as far as Mount Warrigal—you know, being a former cop yourself, this whole idea was bad right from the start."

"I agree," replied Nash. "But we can't do much about that now, can we?"

Morrow sighed. "You're right. Do you know how many people are reported missing each year? Roughly thirty-eight thousand. Around half are young people. Most are found within six months. Some, never."

"Why are you telling me this, Vic?" Nash asked.

"I just want you to know what you're up against. It's a big country out there."

"I'm well aware of that fact, remember? What happened after Mount Warrigal?"

The waitress brought out their pizzas and sat them on the table. Morrow waited until she had gone, rearranging his cutlery and water glass before he commenced again. "Nothing. The investigators did their thing, asked questions and came up empty. They just vanished."

"Nobody just vanishes," Nash said, pinning the detective with his stare.

"They did." Morrow nodded and wiped his mouth with a paper napkin.

"How much do you know about the other girls who went missing?" Nash asked.

"Went missing different times, killed in different ways. Mary first, Peggy next, and lastly Grace Townsend. At first it was thought that Peggy's boyfriend might have been—"

"Wait. Peggy was backpacking with her boyfriend?" Nash asked interrupting.

"Yes. He's still missing. Some theories have him doing it and then wandering off into the desert to die."

"I missed that."

"It was kept out of the papers because he was a suspect, and they didn't want to scare him off. It wasn't let out of the bag until a few weeks later."

"What kind of idiot idea was that?"

Morrow spread his hands apart in a show of helplessness. "Not my doing."

"Was there anything to link the cases?"

"Not as far as they could tell."

"What about the canine saliva?"

"Wild dogs. Plenty of them out there."

"The bites weren't tested to see if they came from the same dog?" Nash asked.

"No need to? Not the same killer."

Nash could feel his anger burning deep within him. "Do you think it might have been a good idea?"

"Not my doing?"

Fuck me.

"You going to eat your pizza?" Morrow asked. "They're bloody good from here."

"Can you tell me how many people go missing up that

highway each year?" Nash asked.

"Two, three, maybe."

"And no one has done anything about it?"

"There have been a few operations."

"What happened?"

"I'm not going to discuss police operations with you, Nash."

Nash tried a different tack. "You do know that killers evolve, right? Shot, bludgeoned, and then strangled."

"I am aware of that. But as I told you, there was nothing to link them at all."

"Except for the *fucking* dog," Nash hissed. He held up his hands as Morrow glared at him. "Sorry, but this is personal."

"I can understand that."

Nash said, "I talked to a reporter who is of the same opinion as me. Something isn't right. She also told me about an Aboriginal girl up near Newman. Molly Wallace."

Morrow nodded. "Hit by a truck. She ran out onto the road. Driver said he thought she was being chased by a wild dog. Poor girl had no chance."

"Was the driver from interstate?"

"No. Meekatharra. He's not driving anymore. Hitting that kid shot his nerves."

"Do you know his name?" Nash asked.

Morrow stared at him and for a moment Nash thought he wasn't going to tell him. "Jim Hanson."

Suddenly hungry, Nash realised he hadn't eaten any pizza. He took a couple of bites and then asked, "So let me get this straight, there is no reason to believe that there is a possible serial killer working the Great Northern Highway?"

"No evidence," Morrow said, correcting Nash.

"What do you mean by that?"

"There is no evidence linking them to suggest that this is the work of one killer. But I'm not saying that we don't think it. We work in facts, remember. And there are none."

"Shit."

"I wish you luck, Nash, I really do." He leaned down, coming up with a briefcase. He opened it and took out a file. "I could get into deep shit for giving you this, Nash."

He paused briefly as though contemplating his next move before passing it across the table. Nash took it quickly then opened it and saw that it was a police file. His gaze snapped up in surprise.

"Don't worry, they're not originals. But if you get caught with them, I swear to God I'll say they were stolen." Morrow closed the briefcase and returned it to the floor, taking a mouthful of water from his glass then wiping his lips with a serviette.

"Why?" Nash asked, fixing him with a concerned look.

"Consider it a favour to a colleague."

"But I'm not—"

"Deep down you are."

Nash thanked him and closed it up.

"Where do you figure to start?" Morrow asked him.

"Right where the trail ran out. Mount Warrigal."

CHAPTER SIX

PERTH
WESTERN AUSTRALIA

Nash had the file spread across his bed. In it were pictures of the victims. Mary Allen was 22 and the first to be found back in 2010. According to the report she'd been shot with a large caliber bullet not found in the body.

Her corpse had been found off the side of the highway north of Mount Warrigal. She'd obviously been there for a while because what was left of her had been ravaged by animals. The heat and flies had sped up decomposition and the pictures were not pretty.

The next one to be found was Peggy Lester. She was a 19-year-old from Adelaide in South Australia. She'd been backpacking with her boyfriend, Pete Rogers. He, too, was from South Australia and like Peggy was also 19. Like Morrow had said, there was no presence of him in the file anywhere else.

Peggy had been killed by blunt force trauma. The likely weapon according to the medical examiner was a crowbar or a heavy pipe? Her body had been found just north of Meekatharra. Again, off the side of the highway, but in a dry creek bed. The state of her body had not been as decomposed as the other. It had been spotted by a truck driver as he drove across the dry waterway. That was in 2015.

The only other outstanding note from the medical examiner was that the body had on it numerous bite marks from what was thought to have been a dog.

The third girl was Grace Townsend. Hailing from Perth, Grace was discovered in August 2019, just west of Wiluna; the town famous for being the end of the Canning Stock Route.

The route—created by a man called Alfred Canning in 1908 for use by the Kimberley cattlemen taking their stock south to market—had around 51 wells dotted along its length which spanned just over two-thousand kilometers from Halls Creek to Wiluna.

What Grace was doing out there, no one knew. She was originally traveling to Darwin from her home in Perth. The assumption was that the killer picked her up off the highway and took her out on the deserted gravel road until he could kill her without any interruptions. This theory, however, could not explain away the dog bites on her legs.

Grace had been 21.

Surprisingly, Morrow had included the last girl, Molly Wallace, killed in 2016. The Aboriginal girl who lived in Bennelong, a town just off the Great Northern Highway, had been killed fifty kilometers north towards Newman.

Her death was ruled misadventure. But once again, there

was the presence of bites from dogs on her legs. Coupled with a report from the truck driver it was quite possible that she was being chased by wild dogs when she ran onto the highway. But no one would ever know.

Although the questions remained, why was she so far north? And why was she naked?

Nash flicked back through the reports to check on the other girls. Like Molly Wallace, all three had been lacking clothes. That was a common link along with the dog bites, barring the first victim.

Then something dawned on Nash; he hurriedly looked at the pictures once more. All the girls apart from the first one had bite marks on their legs. Wild dogs would have gone for the throat tearing and ripping to bring down their prey. The victims would have had defensive wounds on their arms. These weren't wild dogs. These dogs were trained. The girls were hunted.

Nash leaned back and let out a slow breath. Things had just gone from bad to worse.

Nash looked at his watch and did a quick calculation of what the time would be back in Emerald. He thought screw it, then took out his phone and hit speed dial.

"Hello?"

"Hi, baby. It's me."

"Nash? What time is it?" Gloria sounded tired. He guessed he'd woken her up.

"Sorry, Gloria, I just needed to talk to someone."

"It's alright, babe. Just give me a minute." He heard her talking in the background low, soft. "OK, what did you want to talk about?"

"Is my baby girl in there with you?"

"Would she be anywhere else?"

"I talked to the police officer in charge tonight. Well, not quite in charge. He was liaison to the detectives who investigated the disappearance."

"How did it go?" Gloria asked.

"I'm not sure."

"What do you mean you're not sure?"

He told her about the conversation they had over the pizza and then about the file that Morrow had given him. "It's like they know something is bad out there, but they can't investigate it unless they can join the dots."

"Then maybe you've come along at the right time, Dave. Maybe he's hoping you can join those dots for them."

"Yes, at the expense of my niece."

"What did you find in the files?" Gloria asked.

"I'm not sure and maybe I'm reading too much into it, but…"

"But what?"

"I think these girls were hunted."

Gloria was shocked. "Why would you say that?"

"They only have wounds from the dogs on their legs. There are no defensive wounds on their arms or not even a ripping of the throat. Not like if wild dogs were going after them."

"Oh God, Dave, I hope you're wrong."

"So do I, Gloria, but I don't think I am."

"Are you going to call your brother and let him know what you found out?"

Dave thought about it for a moment and then decided that he wouldn't. "No, this is something they don't need to know about."

"I agree. Where to now?"

"I'm going to head north tomorrow," Dave replied. "They were last seen at Mount Warrigal. Going to ask a few questions around there, see what I can find out. Also, I want to have a talk to a truck driver at Meekatharra. He was the one who hit the Aboriginal girl."

"Alright, Dave, you be careful. Call me when you need to. I'll be here. We'll both be here."

"I'm sorry, Gloria. I haven't even asked you how your day has been."

"It's all right. Honest. Just take care of yourself."

Nash's phone beeped. He looked at the screen. The damn thing was just about flat.

"I have to go. Love you."

"Love you, too."

ADELAIDE
SOUTH AUSTRALIA

Red and blue lights strobed off the surrounding houses in the middle of suburbia. Detective Sergeant Randall Brewer walked slowly along the street to the center of all the activity. Already one of his team was on the scene, Cassidy Palmer. He found her talking to a uniformed officer outside the gate of the house in question. "What do we have, Cass?" Brewer asked.

Palmer was in her early thirties with long dark hair tied

back in a ponytail. She looked tired and he noted she still had on the pantsuit he'd seen her in earlier in the day.

She let out a long sigh. "It's a fucking mess. Both victims were tortured. The man more than the woman. But still…"

Brewer looked at the entrance to the home as one of the bodies was brought out. His expression turned grim. "Do we have a name?"

"Daniel and Amy Nash."

"Any idea who was responsible?"

"Not one. Neighbours neither saw nor heard anything."

"Did you run their names to see if they were known to the system?"

Palmer nodded. "They are clean if you discount the odd speeding ticket. However, a couple of weeks ago their daughter and her boyfriend were reported missing. Investigation is still open."

"Where was that?" Brewer asked.

"Western Australia."

Brewer nodded. "See if you can track down any other next of kin."

"There is one. A brother. Name of David."

"Have you notified him yet?"

"Just keep getting voice mail. I left a message to call me but so far, nothing."

"Anyone else?"

"A Gloria Browning. Same address in Queensland."

"Call her, she might know something or at least be able to put us in contact with the brother."

"Will do."

Gloria's phone buzzed angrily on the nightstand beside the bed. She rolled over and answered it with a tired, "Senior Constable Browning."

"Gloria Browning?"

"That's me."

"I'm Detective Cassidy Palmer from the Adelaide Homicide Squad."

That got her attention. Gloria was wide awake now. "What can I do for you, Detective?"

Rachel shifted beside her in the bed. Gloria placed a calming hand on her back, and she stilled.

"Did I hear you say Senior Constable?"

"You did. I work for Queensland Police."

"Fine, fine. I'm looking for David Nash. He is a relation to you?"

"We live in a de facto relationship. Why?"

"Is he there? I tried his phone, but no one answered."

Gloria was starting to worry. "He's in Perth. His sister-in-law called and asked if he could help find his niece. He was in Adelaide—" she looked at the clock. 2am. "The day before yesterday. Is there something wrong?"

"I really need to speak to him—"

"Tell me, damn it," Gloria's voice went up. "I'm a police

officer. You can tell me."

There was a drawn-out silence before Palmer said, "It's about his brother and sister-in-law. They were murdered this evening."

"Oh, no," Gloria gasped, her emotions whirling in her head.

"I'm sorry. As you can see it's important that we can get hold of him."

"Don't worry, Detective. I'll inform Dave and have him call you."

"He can reach me at—"

But Gloria had switched off. How the hell was she going to tell Dave this?

PERTH
WESTERN AUSTRALIA

Nash was stunned by the news. He sat on the edge of the bed and seemed numb, unable to speak. "I'm so sorry, Dave," Gloria said to him again.

He attempted to speak but couldn't. He cleared his throat and tried again. "Do—do they know who?"

"No. Listen, I'll fly down and meet you in Adelaide. OK?"

Nash found himself saying, "No. I'm not going back."

"But, Dave—"

"No, Gloria. The best thing I can do is to find Tiffany."

"You're not thinking straight—"

"I'm thinking fine," he snapped, cutting her off. A pause,

silence. "I'm sorry, Gloria. That was no way to speak to you."

"It's all right, Dave. It's all come as a shock to you."

He sat there on the edge of the bed staring at the grey carpet beneath his feet.

"Are you really serious about not going to Adelaide, Dave?" Gloria asked him.

"I think so, babe. If there is any chance that Tiffany is still alive, I need to keep looking."

"You know there's a chance that she and her boyfriend are..." She let her voice trail away.

"If they are then maybe I can find the person responsible, so it doesn't happen to anyone else."

"All right, Dave. I'll head down to Adelaide and see what I can find out. You keep looking."

"What about Rach?" he asked her.

"I'll leave her with my sister. Besides, they've got a new puppy. Rachel will love it to death—oh shit, sorry."

"Don't worry," Nash said, and a faint smile touched his lips as he pictured Rachel with the poor creature tucked under her arm, carrying it around the house. "Poor dog."

"Yes."

"I love you, Gloria."

"Love you, too, Dave. Take care and I'll call you once I get to Adelaide."

The line went dead, and Nash remained on the edge of the bed staring at the floor. He felt his emotions start to well up and for a moment he wished he had Gloria with him. He shook it off and dialed the number Gloria had given him for the detective.

It was answered after a couple of rings. "Detective Palmer."

"Detective, this is Dave Nash. My...partner told me to call you."

"Yes, Mr. Nash. I gather she told you what was happening?"

"She did."

"I'm sorry for your loss, Mr.—"

"Call me, Dave."

"Sorry for your loss, Dave."

"Thank you."

"When can we expect you back in Adelaide? I have a few things we need to go over."

"I'm not coming," he replied.

"I don't think you understand, we need to talk to you. You were one of the last people to see them."

"I understand perfectly, Detective. But I'm still not coming. I have something else to take care of."

"Your niece?"

"That's right. I'm leaving soon to head north. So, if you have questions, ask them now."

"This is highly unusual considering the circumstances."

"Ask them, Detective, or hang up."

Palmer sighed. "You spent time with them, right?"

"Yes."

"How were they?"

"Worried about their daughter."

"As they would be," Palmer said. "Did they have any enemies that you know of?"

"I don't think so. If they did, I'm sure that I would be the last to know."

"Your relationship with them wasn't the best?" Palmer asked.

"Mainly with my brother," Nash replied.

"Yet he called you to help find his daughter."

"Not exactly."

"Oh?"

"It was Amy who called."

"Not your brother then?"

Nash shook his head. "No. Things are a little bit—were a little bit testy there."

"Why was that?" Palmer asked.

"Because of something that happened with my previous employment," Nash explained.

"What did that happen to be?"

"I shot four people."

Palmer went quiet for a moment and Nash figured she was mulling over the information that he just given her. Before she could say anything or ask a question, he said, "If you did your research, you'll know that I was an undercover cop."

"I haven't got that far into you yet," Palmer told him. "Gloria didn't mention it either. All this was meant to be a death notification and to have you come to Adelaide to answer some questions."

"Well, now you know," Nash replied. "My brother wanted nothing to do with me after that. No—not true, it was when I was undercover with a gang of outlaw bikers. Shit hit the fan there as well. That was when it all started."

"I'll have to look into that as well." She sighed. "If you're not coming back, can I trust you to be contactable?"

He looked at his watch. "I'm headed north today, and I don't know what the reception will be like. Gloria is headed to Adelaide, so you'll be able to talk to her. I'm sure between the two of you you'll be able to get hold of me."

"As I said this is highly unusual." She sighed again. "Again, I'm sorry for your loss, Dave. Good morning."

"Thank you, Detective."

The line went dead, and Nash lay back on his bed, closing his eyes. He thought there would be tears by now but maybe they would come later. After another ten minutes his breathing slowed, and he went to sleep.

CHAPTER SEVEN

DRAYTON
WESTERN AUSTRALIA

There wasn't much to Drayton although it was just a couple of hundred kilometers north of Perth. Besides the usual outback offerings of heat, flies, and dust, it boasted a couple of roadhouses, some old rundown shops, a pub, a museum, and very few houses that seemed to dwindle each year.

The locals called it Drytown because that's exactly what it was. Arid, hot, and a bastard of a place to live. Yet here they were.

Nash finished filling the Commodore with fuel and replaced the cap. He walked across the hot concrete towards the double automatic doors and felt the cool air hit him in the face when they slid open; instant relief from the already skyrocketing temperature outside.

Walking up to the counter, he was greeted by a chubby-faced young attendant who grinned at him. "Hot enough for ya?"

"You know what they say," Nash replied.

"Yeah, burn the balls off a kangaroo."

Nash gave a wry smile. It was wrong but he wasn't about to correct her.

"That'll be sixty bucks."

He tapped his card and waited for the beep before removing it. "You worked here long?"

"Year, maybe."

"You get many backpackers, hitchhikers through here?"

"Loads, ay." She passed over the receipt.

Nash reached into his pocket. He withdrew a photo and asked the cashier, "You ever seen her before?"

She curled a lip. "Nah."

"You sure?"

She frowned. "Maybe, yeah. I think a couple of coppers came in asking about her and a friend. Come to think of it."

"But you've never seen her before?"

"Nuh."

"Thank you."

He left behind the blessed relief of the air-conditioned roadhouse and out into the heat. Nash wasn't sure why he'd even bothered to ask; he already knew that the last confirmed sighting of Tiffany was Mount Warrigal.

Nash climbed into the Commodore and before driving off picked up his map and looked at it. Two-hundred kilometers up the road was another roadhouse. On the map it was marked as Keller Creek. It looked a likely spot to stop for the night. To push it any further was probably a step too far the way he felt. He'd hit Mount Warrigal fresh tomorrow and ask around.

Starting the vehicle, Nash put it into drive, and drove away from the roadhouse.

GREAT NORTHERN HIGHWAY
WESTERN AUSTRALIA

It was a landscape of endless red dirt and sparse scrub as far as the eye could see. The two most dangerous things Nash had encountered so far were the bodies of giant Red Kangaroos killed by passing road trains, and fatigue, the monotony of the endless strip of asphalt creating a hypnotic effect and his eyes began their steady creep towards closed from concentrating so hard.

The odd caravan and road train were welcome relief coming in the opposite direction but other than that the journey was surprisingly bland.

He figured another twenty minutes and Keller Creek would come into view through the rising heatwaves rippling off the highway.

At first it looked as though the heat was playing tricks on his eyes but as he got closer, he made out the two figures walking alongside the asphalt. "Of all the stupid—" he started to growl.

He pressed his foot on the brake and brought the Commodore to a stop beside the hitchers. One male, one female. Their faces beneath the fly netting on their brimmed hats looked to be redder than boiled beetroot.

The male opened the passenger door. He was young, maybe twenty-two. "You give ride?"

His English was terrible. "Mate, what the fuck are you doing walking all the way out here?"

He gave a friendly smile and said, "Going Moppit Station?"

Nash frowned. "Moppit Station?"

The young man shook his head. "Moppit. Moppit Station."

"Moppit Station?"

Again, he shook his head and this time he pulled out a map, opening it and putting it on the seat. He stabbed it with his finger. "Moppit."

Nash looked at it. The name said Moffat Station. It was north and west of Mount Warrigal. He looked at the young man and nodded. "Get in. I'm going to Mount Warrigal."

The guy looked relieved and turned to his friend, rattling off some words in a language Nash didn't understand. The pair opened the rear door and climbed in, him in the front, and her, along with their backpacks in the back seat.

Moments later, Nash was back on the road. "What are your names?"

"Werner and Emma."

"Werner and Emma?"

"Yes."

"I'm Dave."

"Dave?"

"That's it. What are you doing out here?"

"Go to work."

"Work? On the station?"

Werner nodded. "Yes. Earn money before we go on."

Nash nodded. "You know it is dangerous to hitch out here, right?"

"What?"

"Walking. Dangerous."

Werner shook his head. "Australia? No. Not dangerous."

Nash shook his head. Whatever these people had heard about Australia being safe was a fallacy.

From the back seat, Emma said something in her native tongue. Werner answered her back.

"What did she say?"

Werner chuckled. "She said I hope he isn't a mad killer."

"Tell her she is safe. I used to be a policeman."

"Policeman? Really?" Werner seemed surprised. He turned his head and repeated what he'd just learned. Nash looked in the rearview mirror and saw that Emma seemed relieved and satisfied with what she'd just heard.

Twenty minutes later, as predicted, Keller Creek came into view. "I'm stopping here for the night."

Werner nodded. "We keep going."

Nash shook his head. "No. Stay here and I'll take you to Mount Warrigal tomorrow."

He relayed the message to his friend. She nodded. "Ja."

"All right. Thank you."

"Where are you from?"

"Germany. Stuttgart."

"Cool."

Nash swung off the highway and into the driveway of the roadhouse. The main building had a large restaurant, which doubled as a pub, attached to it. Out the back was a line of small accommodation blocks.

Nash parked and they climbed out. They went inside and found a tired looking man behind the counter. Nash said, "You got a couple of spare dongers out the back?"

"Sure."

"How much?"

"Fifty for the night for a single, sixty for a double."

He looked at Werner who seemed happy with the price. "We'll take them. What time does the restaurant close?"

"They usually stop cooking about eight," the man replied as he handed over a couple of keys. "Just need you to fill out the register."

"No computer?"

He shook his head. "Too unreliable."

Nash filled out the register and placed the pen down, but before he stepped aside, he ran his finger down the list.

"Looking for something, Mister?"

"Yes, a name."

"You'll find plenty of them there."

The former undercover took out his picture of Tiffany. "You see her before?"

The man stared hard at the photo, his eyes narrowing. Then surprisingly, he nodded. "Sure. Her and her friend stayed out back in five."

"You sure?"

"Never forget a face."

Nash pushed the register aside so Emma could fill it out. The attendant's eyes drifted to the German woman and lingered for longer than necessary. Nash frowned and looked to his right. For the first time since picking both backpackers up, he got a good look at her. Like her partner, she had dark hair, except hers was tied back in a ponytail. Apart from being a little redder than normal from the harsh Australian sun, her face seemed flawless. However, it wasn't her face that the man was looking at. She wore a green, sleeveless tank top with nothing else underneath. Her breasts were of average size, but her nipples were hard and erect, straining to burst through the fabric.

Nash rolled his eyes. "Hey, I'm over here."

"What?"

"Did they seem all right to you?"

"Definitely," the man replied with a smile.

"Hey! The girl and her partner? Did they seem all right?"

"Huh? Yeah, yeah. There was one little issue but nothing major."

"What little issue?"

"Nothing much, like I said. Pete and Jimmy Nolan. Couple of brothers who hunt roos. They travel up and down the highway all the time."

"Tell me about it."

"Nothing to tell."

Nash's stare hardened. "I'm interested."

"Okay. They were eating dinner in the pub and the brothers came in. One of them said something and the bloke who was with the girl took offense to it. They had words and that was it."

"What did he say?"

The man glanced nervously at Emma. "Ahh—"

"What did he say?" Nash asked again.

"Ah—nice tits."

Nash nodded. He picked the key up and said, "Thanks." Then he left.

"You need to pay," the man called after him.

"Yeah, in the morning."

The accommodation unit was stifling. The hot air greeting Nash as he stepped inside forced him to pause. He reached around the door jamb and turned on the air conditioning unit which started to force all the hot air out immediately.

He stepped inside and tossed his bag on the bed then sat beside it. Nash moaned. The door was still open and there was no way he felt like getting up to shut it. Besides, the cool air from the unit overhead was blowing on him.

He closed his eyes and was almost asleep when a soft voice said, "Excuse me."

Nash opened his eyes and sat up. Emma was standing in the doorway. It was the first time he'd heard her speak English and had reached the conclusion that she couldn't. "Hey, what's up?"

"Our room. You look at it?"

Nash was confused. "Is there something wrong?"

"Come, you look."

With a frustrated sigh, Nash dragged himself off the bed and followed her to her unit. He followed her in and stopped. The place was disgusting. The bed was unmade, the sheets stained, rubbish uncollected. "Where is Werner?" Nash asked.

"He go see man."

Nash turned and looked outside and saw Werner coming towards them. His demeanor told Nash all he needed to know. The young German said, "Er ist ein verdammtes Arschloch."

"What?"

"Sorry. He's a fucking asshole."

"What did he say?"

"He said there was nothing else. Take or leave."

Nash looked around the parking area. Apart from his Commodore, there was nothing else. "Wait here."

The man glanced up and backpedaled when he saw Nash coming for him. He held up his hands and blurted out, "Now wait—"

The former undercover grabbed a fistful of shirt and almost dragged the man across the counter. "Listen up, you fucking wanker. I'm tired and cranky and in no mood for your bullshit. Give them a clean room or I'll bury you out the back somewhere."

"I told the German bloke I had nothing else."

"Don't lie. Get another key or you're fucked."

"Okay, okay."

Nash let him go. The man got another key and gave it to him. "That'll be—"

"Fuck off."

When Nash walked outside his phone rang. Retrieving it from his pocket, he checked the display and hit the answer key. "Hey, babe."

"Hey yourself," came Gloria's soft voice. "How are you doing?"

"Fine. Tired."

"Where are you?"

"Some place called Keller Creek. I had to stop. Couldn't go on. Where are you?"

"Just touched down in Adelaide. I have a meeting with the detective later this evening."

"Let me know how it goes."

"Of course."

"How was my girl when you left?"

"There were tears at first and then she saw the puppy. By the time I left it was the puppy that was crying."

Nash smiled. "Miss you, babe."

"Miss you, too, Nash. I've got to go. Talk tonight."

"Sure, bye."

He disconnected the call and smiled as he thought about Rachel. He was right, the puppy would need a therapist by the time Gloria returned home.

He walked back to the donger and found the two backpackers standing outside. He held out the key for Emma. "How?"

"He saw the error of his ways."

"Huh?"

Werner rattled off something in German and she smiled. "Thank you."

"That's all right."

Werner nodded. "We buy you dinner tonight?"

"You don't have to do that."

"Yes."

He seemed determined so Nash agreed. "Sure, why not?"

"Good. See you at seven?"

Nash looked at his watch. It was four. Time for a short sleep and a shower before they ate. "Yes. I'll be there."

Nash felt little better after the short sleep. The cold shower, on the other hand, picked him up. Until he stepped outside, and the cloying heat slapped him down again.

"Shit a frigging brick," he growled.

He looked along the row of dongers and saw that Werner and Emma had the same idea as he did.

Out on the highway a road train with four trailers roared past whipping up the red dust into a rising plume. Behind it a few hundred meters came an Isuzu D-Max 4X4 towing a caravan. Its indicator came on and it pulled off the blacktop and into the roadhouse parking area.

"How are you feeling?" Nash asked the German pair.

"Hungry," Emma replied.

"Then let's get something to eat."

There were more vehicles parked outside the roadhouse

now. Mostly 4X4s. As they walked inside, the first thing that hit Nash was the aroma of cooking food. His stomach growled.

He looked up at the chalk menu board and decided on a steak. It came with roast vegetables and gravy. Sounded good to him.

Emma and Werner ordered their meals, and then they ordered and waited for drinks before joining Nash at his table. Nash had a beer which was cold and tasted good. While they waited, they talked. Mostly about Germany.

Suddenly the sound of raucous laughter foretold the approach of two men. The door opened and sure enough, two dirty, unshaven men entered the restaurant/pub. They paused inside the door and looked around.

Their eyes lingered on the table where Nash and his two new acquaintances sat. One more so than the other. He was a shorter man with a silver scar that ran down his heavily stubbled left cheek starting at his eye which was a milky white color.

His friend grabbed his arm and said something that Nash didn't hear, and they both went to the bar where they ordered beers.

Nash's attention was drawn by the approach of the waitress bringing their meals. By the time he was halfway through the food on his plate, he had to admit that it was right up there with some of the better pub meals he'd partaken of over the years.

When he was finally done, Nash felt like another beer.

"You two want more drinks?"

Werner nodded and looked at Emma who said, "Sure."

Nash went up to the bar, keeping a reasonable distance between him and the other drinkers.

While waiting for his drinks he heard a voice crackle, "Nice bit of scruff you have at the table."

Knowing that the words were directed at him, he chose to ignore them.

"Hey, bloke, I'm talking to you."

Nash looked in the direction the words came from. It was the short scruffy man with the scarred face. It had to be.

"I said that you have—"

"I heard you," Nash's words were curt.

"Does she give good head?"

Once more Nash chose to ignore him, turning away to face the bar.

"I bet she does. With them lips my guess is she'd suck a golf ball through a garden hose."

"Leave it, Jimmy," the other man said.

A light bulb went on in Nash's head. Jimmy and Pete Nolan.

"Shut up, Pete. I'm only having some fun."

When the drinks arrived, Nash paid for them, collected his change then picked up the glasses and carried them across to the table. He eyed Werner and Emma who waited patiently, then grinned at them before placing the drinks on the scarred top in front of each. Nash was about to sit when he heard Jimmy again.

"Show us your tits, love."

Nash glanced at the two Germans. Werner asked, "What he say?"

The former undercover shook his head. "Nothing. I'll be right back."

He turned and walked towards the two brothers; all eyes were on him now and the room had gone suddenly silent. "Ooh, look at him, Pete. The man has gone and got all heated up. Looks scary."

"Do you practice at this, or does it just come naturally?" Nash asked Jimmy.

"What?"

"Being an asshole. Do you practice?"

Pete laughed out loud until his brother glared at him with his good eye. "Mister, you aren't being very friendly."

"I'm not here to make friends. So, let me give you some advice. You either treat the lady with respect or I'll come back over here and break your fucking neck."

Rage shot through Jimmy, but it was Pete who stopped him from doing something stupid. He grabbed his brother's arm and said, "Not now, Jimmy."

Nash turned and left them, walking back to the table. Behind him he heard Jimmy say, "I'm going to kill that prick, Pete."

"Shut up and drink your beer," his brother responded.

"Is everything all right?" Werner asked.

"It's fine."

They talked some more and when Nash finished his beer he said, "That's me. I'm turning in for the night."

Werner said, "We might have one more drink."

The former undercover knew it was a bad idea, but he left it at that. He wasn't their guardian. So he stood up and left.

Back in the room, Nash looked at his watch. It was eight o'clock. He reached for his cell and dialed. A few rings later a voice said, "Hello?"

"Hello, Grace."

"Dave?" asked Gloria's sister.

"Yeah. Is she awake?"

"What do you think? I swear you and Gloria have her on permanent recharge."

"Her batteries will run dry soon," he told her with a smile.

"She is so sweet, Dave. I haven't got the heart to scold her. And the poor puppy…"

"Let it bite her, that'll slow her down."

"Nooo," she gasped. "I couldn't do that. I'll get her for you."

"Thanks."

A few minutes later and Rachel exploded onto the phone. "Daddy!"

"Hey, baby girl. Are you alright?"

"I'm good. Guess what?"

"What?"

"Aunt Grace has a puppy. His name is Barry, but she calls him Traumatized. Why would she do that?"

Nash grinned. "I don't know, sweetie."

"When are you coming home?" she asked.

"In a little while. I've still got some things to do first."

"OK. Don't rush. I can keep playing with Barry."

"Okay."

"Can I have a puppy when you get home?"

Nash winced. "You'll have to ask mummy."

"Do you think she'll say yes?"

"I don't know. Can you put Aunt Grace back on?"

"Sure."

"Now, when you say goodbye, teeth and then bed. Right?"

"Aw, Dad—"

"Right?"

"Okay."

"Love you."

"Love you, too. Good night."

"Night."

"I'm here, Dave."

"Traumatized?"

"Definitely."

"Are you going to be okay with her?" Nash asked.

"Don't worry, we'll be fine."

"Okay. Thanks for looking after my girl. Bye."

"Bye, Dave. Take care."

The call ended and Nash undressed and climbed into bed and closed his eyes.

CHAPTER EIGHT

ADELAIDE
SOUTH AUSTRALIA

"Gloria Browning."

"Cassidy Palmer," the detective responded.

"Pleased to meet you."

"Likewise."

They sat down at a table inside the restaurant and picked up menus. "Shall we order before we talk shop?" Palmer asked.

"Why not? I'm starving."

After a few minutes, they'd decided on what they wanted and called the waitress over. The harried girl waved a response as she finished with another customer before heading for their table. She was attired in standard hospitality black and white.

The restaurant was dimly lit with mood lighting and had artificial plants scattered around the dining area. Once they had ordered, Palmer said, "I've done some checking on you.

Sorry, old habit. Your record speaks for itself."

"My wild days."

"I also see that Dave Nash was part of those days as well."

"You're talking about the outlaw motorcycle gang?"

"Yes."

"Like I said, crazy days."

"Have you heard from Dave at all?" Palmer asked.

"I called him when I landed."

"Any progress?"

"Nothing to write home about. What can you tell me about the deaths of Dave's brother and sister-in-law?"

"Not a lot at the moment except the fact it looks like they were tortured before they were killed."

Gloria raised her eyebrows. "Tortured?"

"Afraid so. Can you think of any reason someone might want to do that?"

She shook her head. "No, we never—Dave never—had much to do with them after—well let's say because of what happened with his job."

"Dave did say that."

"Do you have any idea who is responsible?" Gloria asked.

"No. There is a witness who saw a man walking towards their door at the right time but couldn't give us a thorough description."

"What did they see?"

"I can't really tell—"

"Come on, Palmer, we're both coppers."

"Male, Caucasian, solid, possibly with dark hair."

Gloria shook her head. "That could be anyone."

"Isn't that the truth?"

"Did you dig into their background?"

Palmer nodded. "We found nothing. Squeaky clean. Nothing at all set off any alarm bells."

"Random?"

"No. My partner and I think they were tortured for a reason. Which leads me to this. Looking at Dave's record he's made a lot of enemies. Can you think of any one of them who stands out?"

Gloria thought for a moment and then another moment.

"Anyone recent?"

"Oh, shit!" she exclaimed.

"What?"

"There was that thing up the bush, but…"

"But what?"

"I'm thinking of someone else."

"Who?"

"Betty O'Malley. Dave killed both of her sons."

"I read about that. That would piss you off," Palmer agreed. "I would say she's just shot to the top of the list. The woman may be in jail but from what I've read about her it wouldn't make her stop."

Gloria agreed. "No, that woman is evil. They killed one of mine in front of us. Dave snapped when he saw it happen and took down four of her people. Her sons included."

"He sounds like a capable man."

"When he's backed into a corner, and the chips are down,

there's no one better. Trust me, I've seen him in action."

"From what I've read, I tend to agree with you."

There was a brief silence before Gloria asked, "Are you thinking that whoever did this could be after Dave?"

"It's a possibility, although it might be too early to tell."

"I'll warn him anyway."

"You do that."

KELLER CREEK
WESTERN AUSTRALIA

Who the hell was playing drums at this time of the night? Nash thought as he came out of his sleep.

It took a few moments longer for him to realize what it actually was. Someone was pounding frantically on his door. He swung his legs over the edge of the bed and sat there still half asleep. "Who is it?"

"Help, you must help us, Dave."

It was a woman's voice. "Emma?"

"Yes, they are killing him."

Hurriedly, Nash pulled on his jeans not worrying about his shirt. Then he slipped his feet into his shoes before hurrying to the door. He opened it and found an agitated Emma on the other side. "Hurry, please."

She ran ahead of him, and it wasn't long before he could hear the cheers of the crowd and the cries of pain.

When they rounded the corner of the building, there they were. The small crowd, Werner, and the two Nolan brothers.

"Fuck me," Nash growled and closed in on the group.

Werner was about out on his feet and each time he went down they dragged him back up to do it all over again.

Nash looked around and saw a ute with equipment in the back of it. He glanced in and saw a long-handled shovel. He pulled it out and stomped on it just above the blade so when it snapped, he was left with a shortened handle in his grasp.

Now he was ready to resolve the problem and continued the rest of the way.

As he walked past the crowd the noise suddenly dropped off.

Nash was mad so it probably was a good thing he didn't get his hands on a gun. If he had, things probably would have gone a whole lot worse.

The first thing the Nolan brothers knew that something wasn't right was the audible woosh of the handle displacing air as it gathered speed. Then came the crack like a baseball impacting the bat at almost a hundred miles per hour.

Jimmy Nolan was unaware of what hit him. He dropped like a stone and never moved.

"What the fuck?" Pete cried out, letting Werner go. He whirled on Nash and blurted out, "What did you do that for?"

"Because he's a prick," Nash said and swung the handle once more.

Lights out.

Nash helped Werner to his feet. "Are you alright?"

"I will live," he grunted.

The former undercover could see in the light cast by the roadhouse that he was bleeding from his nose and a cut above his left eye. "Get Emma to see to the cut."

"Hey, who do you think you are?" a large man asked, stepping forward from the group of onlookers. "This was nothing to do with you, *mate*."

Nash was still in no mood for bullshit and squared his shoulders. "You obviously want some so come ahead."

The big man took another step and Nash braced himself. His opponent looked to be the size of a truck, but he wasn't about to back down. Besides, he was too pissed.

He was just about to load up for another swing when blue and red lights strobed off the surrounding area and the short burst of a police siren split the desert night. The white, marked, Land Cruiser rolled to a slow stop and the engine shut down. The lights went out and a middle-aged man with a trim beard and stocky build climbed from the driver's seat. "What's going on here?" His voice was gravelly, disinterested.

"This bloke here put Jimmy and Pete Nolan down with a shovel handle," the big man said. "You need to arrest him, Davis."

"Is that right, SH? Nothing I haven't thought of myself. What were they doing?"

"Nothing."

"You're lying, SH."

"These blokes will back me up." He indicated to the crowd.

"Then what happened to this bloke here?" the police officer asked.

"Fell down."

Davis shook his head. He turned to Nash. "What do you have to say?"

"The two of them were assholes. They decided it would be fun to beat up the backpacker and I showed them the error of their ways. I was just about to show the tree here his when you showed up."

Davis smiled. "That about rings true. SH, get them out of here."

"Are you going to take this bastard's word for it instead of ours, Davis?"

"That's exactly what I'm going to do, now go away before I lock you all up."

"Asshole."

Davis ignored the remark, instead he asked Nash, "What's your name?"

"Dave Nash."

"I'm Sergeant Ben Davis, I run a one-man station in this part of nowhere."

Nash indicated the big man. "SH?"

"Short for Shit Head. I think his real name is Stewart Henry but Shit Head suits. Where are you headed?"

Nash glanced over Davis's shoulder and saw Emma helping Werner away. "I'm headed up to Mount Warrigal."

"Business?"

"Kind of. Looking for a missing girl."

"Relative?"

"Niece."

"Been missing long?"

"Few weeks."

"Name?"

"Tiffany Nash."

Davis recognized the name and nodded. "Had some detectives come through here a while back looking for a girl of that name. She was traveling with some bloke."

"Boyfriend."

"What's your name again?"

"Dave Nash."

Once more the officer's mind started to work. "Are you *that* Dave Nash?"

"Depends on what you mean by 'That'."

"The one who seems to shoot people everywhere he goes."

"Only when they try to shoot me."

Davis chuckled. "Seems to me you do a lot of good. Is there anything you want to ask me?"

"What did you tell the detectives?"

"That I never saw them, but we have a lot of backpackers and hitchers pass through here. I warn them but—"

"Warn them about what?" Nash interrupted.

"I've been out here for ten years," Davis explained. "Left on the end of the vine to rot. It cost me my marriage and my kids. But it's a dangerous place. People go missing all the time."

Nash processed what he'd just been told. For Davis to be posted out here in the middle of nowhere for so long, he must have pissed off the higher ups. Or they thought he was bent but couldn't prove it. "So I've been told."

"If I was you, Nash, I'd go home. That girl you're looking for is most likely buried under three feet of desert or scattered across it by now. I'm sorry but that's the way it is."

Nash understood where he was coming from. "I have to look."

"Of course you do. Good luck."

Davis turned to walk away.

"What about the brothers?" Nash asked.

"They'll sleep it off and I'll talk to them again tomorrow if

I see them."

"Not what I meant," Nash said with a shake of his head. "Did anyone look at them for the disappearances?"

"They're a couple of dumb roo shooters. Too stupid to realize what day it is."

"How long they been out here?"

"Far as I know, all their lives. They travel up and down the highway from here to Newman. Anything else?"

"No."

"Be seeing you, Nash."

"Not if I see you first," Nash muttered.

Davis climbed back into his 4X4 and started the diesel engine. The lights came on and he pulled out of the roadhouse carpark. Once he hit the highway he turned left and disappeared into the darkness.

Nash checked on the German backpackers before going back to his room. Werner would be fine.

His cell rang. He looked at the name and felt a wave of relief. "Hey, babe."

"Hi, Nash."

"What's this Nash business?"

"Just trying it out. I kind of like it."

"I talked to your baby girl earlier."

"Don't you mean your baby girl?" Gloria shot back at him.

"She's all you and you know it."

"How was she?"

"Happy, I think. Driving your sister crazy with all her energy."

"That's Rachel."

There was a moment of silence before Nash asked, "What's

up, Gloria?"

"I talked to Detective Palmer."

"And?" he prompted.

"She said that—that Amy and Danny were tortured by whoever killed them. I'm sorry."

Nash remained silent.

"The Adelaide police think that they did it for information."

"About what?"

"About you."

"Why me?" Nash asked.

"If it's who I think it is, then I think we already know the answer to that," Gloria replied.

Nash stared at the landscape picture on the wall in front of him. It was a gum tree with a fence behind it and a scattering of cows in the background. To the right was a drover on a horse.

"Betty O'Malley," he said without any emotion in his voice.

"That is a real possibility. I'm going to Melbourne tomorrow to question her."

"Be careful, Gloria. If it is her, this might be what the bitch wants."

"If it is her, Dave, then the killer is out there looking for you," she pointed out.

"Shit."

"What is it?"

"They knew I was going to see the reporter."

"You need to warn her, Nash," Gloria urged him. "She could be in danger."

"I'll do it, now. Be careful, Gloria. Love you."

"Love you, too. And you're the one that needs to be careful."

"Hey, I'm Crazy Dave, remember?"

"Yes, but you're not bulletproof. And we need you."

The call disconnected and Nash tried Maria Gallagher. The call went straight to voice mail. "Hi, Maria, Dave Nash. I don't want to alarm you, but you may be in danger. Give me a call and I'll explain everything. Thanks, bye."

With that done Nash suddenly felt tired once more. He took his pants and shoes off and climbed back into bed.

PERTH
WESTERN AUSTRALIA

Joe Black listened to the message again before smashing the phone and disposing of the SIM card. He looked at the terrified figure he had gagged and tied to the chair before him.

Dark lines of mascara had run in rivulets down Maria's cheeks from the gut-wrenching fear and pain that the psychotic killer had already inflicted upon her.

"That didn't take long," Black said. "But it doesn't matter. I'm good at my job."

Maria grunted against her gag.

Black walked over to the nearby table and unfolded a leather bundle, not unlike one a woodworker kept his chisels in. However, this one contained no chisels; there were all types of sharp blades in it. Specialist ones that Black was adept at using.

"I know you told me things, Miss Gallagher. Most of them are probably true." He took out a thin blade and held it in front of her eyes so it was clearly visible. "But you see, I need to be certain of the veracity of your words because once I kill you, there's no coming back to ask a second time is there?"

Once more the crying and screaming started.

He reached out and touched her hand. "Don't worry. It will soon be over."

Twenty minutes later, with the tools of his trade packed up, Joe Black left with all the information he needed to continue his search for Dave Nash.

CHAPTER NINE

**KELLER CREEK
WESTERN AUSTRALIA**

Galahs, dust, heat, and flies. What a quartet to wake up to. The sun hadn't risen that far across the red dirt horizon, and it was already stinking hot. Nash felt beads of sweat already starting to form

A Blue Heeler dog crawled out from under a 4X4 and walked over to him, wagging its tail. Nash patted its head. "You'd best go back, pup. Too hot out here."

The former undercover checked his watch. It was almost seven. He walked along the dongers until he reached the one the German couple were in. He knocked on the door and waited.

When no one answered he tried again.

The door on the next one opened and a man stepped out. "They're gone. Left about an hour ago."

Nash nodded. "Thanks."

He wondered why they would leave without him, after all, he'd said he would take them further. A fly buzzed around his face, and he swatted briskly to wave it away. Back inside the roadhouse, he found the same man who'd been at the counter the previous day. "I'll pay for my night."

He tossed fifty on the counter. The man reached out and grabbed it. "You need to watch your back if you plan on hanging around."

"Why's that?"

"They're not your average troublemakers, the Nolan brothers. There are stories."

"What stories?"

"Just stories."

"Anything specific?" Nash asked.

"Heard one about some station hand going missing after he had a run in with them."

"Really?" Nash sounded almost disinterested.

"True. Word is they buried him between here and Newman."

Nash nodded skeptically. "I'll keep an eye out."

"You do that."

The former undercover turned away and stopped. "How did he get the eye?"

"The bloke that disappeared."

"Uh, huh. Be seeing you."

Outside the temperature continued to rise. Nash climbed into the Commodore and turned the air conditioning up to full. He slipped the shift into reverse and as he looked up, he saw SH Willis staring at him. Nash fixed the man's gaze with his own before giving him a salute and backing out of the park. He then put it into drive, gave Willis the finger, and drove off.

PORT MELBOURNE WOMEN'S CORRECTIONAL FACILITY
VICTORIA

Gloria caught an early morning flight to Tullamarine before hiring a car and heading straight to the prison. At first, she thought that they might not let her see Betty, but apparently someone in charge remembered her and soon after her arrival she was led into a room where she met with the Irish matriarch.

"Well, if it isn't the fecking mole herself," Betty growled.

Gloria gave her a mirthless smile. "Hello, Betty. How's your holiday going? I hope the resort staff are treating you well."

"Fine, lass, just fine. Every day is the same but sometimes you get news. Mostly bad but sometimes some good." Her eyes sparkled as though they were taunting Gloria. "How is that murdering bastard of a husband of yours?"

"He's not my husband, Betty. But he's fine, thank you for asking."

"Must be doing better than I thought then."

"Why is that?"

"Heard he had a death in the family."

Gloria had to hand it to her, the woman wasn't that subtle. "Good news travels fast, huh?"

"Like lightning, love. Now what can I do for you?"

"Nothing really, I just wanted to come visit and look you in the eye."

"Really, what would that be for?"

"Answers."

"Did you get them?"

Gloria nodded. "I do believe I did."

"That's nice."

For a long moment Gloria felt like leaning across the stainless-steel table and slapping the smug expression off Betty O'Malley's face. But that would be getting down to her level. "You think you're tough? You're not so tough."

"Matter of opinion, I guess."

"The Outback Animals bikers were tougher than you. You're just a husk of a woman who lost her sons to crime."

Betty's stare hardened. "I lost my boys because of a murdering copper."

"They got what they deserved."

Betty O'Malley came to her feet. "What would you know, you fecking bitch?"

"I was there, remember? I saw what they did."

"Feck you."

Gloria stood up. She waved her hand in the air and said, "Enjoy your stay, Betty."

As Gloria walked out of the interview room, Betty called

out, "I'm not done yet. I'm not done by a long fecking way, you bitch."

The door slammed shut, leaving the crazy-eyed woman standing there with her nostrils flaring.

Gloria found herself a motel close to the airport and checked in. Her plan was to fly back to Queensland the next day. She ate a salad wrapped in flatbread for lunch before lying back on the bed, flicking the television on. She had tried to ring Nash, but he must have been out of range because his phone went straight to voicemail.

She was only half watching the midday movie when a news headline came on the channel. This one caught her attention. It was a story about a news reporter who'd been found alone in her home in Perth. Tortured before having her throat cut.

Gloria grabbed for the remote to turn it up so she could hear what the news presenter was saying. Then she heard the name. Maria Gallagher. "Oh shit, no."

She reached out and picked up her cell from the bedside stand and hit the speed dial for Nash's phone. Once more, it went to voicemail, but this time she left a more urgent message. "Dave, you need to ring me. He's killed her. He's killed the reporter. Dammit, call me."

When she disconnected, she stared numbly at the television, but the movie had already come back on. Her mind whirled as she tried to process this latest information. Once more, Gloria picked up her phone and dialed a number. She waited for someone to answer and said, "Yes, I need to book a flight to Perth as soon as possible."

MOUNT WARRIGAL
WESTERN AUSTRALIA

Nash arrived in town just after midday. His first port of call was the police station, where he pulled up on the gravel berm out front. When he switched off the ignition, he could feel the heat beaming through the glass of the windows and he knew it was going to be a scorcher when he got out.

Upon opening the door, the cool air was quickly dissipated as hot air rushed in to wrap its suffocating blanket around him. He climbed out, shut the door and walked up onto the footpath. Under his feet, the dust covered asphalt felt soft and squishy, a result of the sun's intensity.

His cell pinged letting him know he had a message. He'd get it after.

The effect was opposite when he opened the police station door. It was the cold air rushing out to greet him. Once inside he was addressed by a young female constable who was manning the counter. "Yes, sir, what can I do for you?"

"I'd like to see your sergeant or whoever's in charge if they're around, please," Nash replied.

She looked at him inquiringly for a moment, but Nash

wasn't forthcoming with any more information. "Might I ask why, sir?"

"It's about a missing person."

"And who is it that is missing?"

He looked at her name badge. It said Constable Eleanor Parker. She was in her early 20s and her long brown hair was tied back into a bun. "My niece."

"And you are?"

Nash reached into his pocket for his identification. He showed her and said, "Dave Nash. Private investigator from Emerald in Queensland."

"Wait here for a moment, please, sir. I'll be right back."

Nash turned away from the counter and looked at a large corkboard screwed to the wall. It was covered in different sheets of paper, but the one that caught his eye was a missing person.

She looked to be about 19 or 20. Blonde hair, the description said she was about 175 centimeters tall. A quick calculation with the date told him she'd been missing for three years and 10 months.

"Mr. Nash, is it?" the man's voice asked.

Nash turned and saw a broad-shouldered sergeant standing behind the counter. "That's me," Nash said.

"I'm Sergeant Halliday. How can I help? My constable said you were here looking for your niece."

"That's right. She's been missing a few weeks now."

"What was the name?"

"Tiffany Nash. She went missing along with her boyfriend. They were hitchhiking."

Halliday nodded slowly. "Yes, I remember. The detectives came here for a while, asked around. Then they moved on."

"I was told that this was where the trail went cold."

"That's right. Your niece and her boyfriend were looking for some work. Apparently, they ran out of money."

"Ran out of money?"

"That's right."

"Who gave the detectives that information?" Nash asked.

"I'd have to check."

"Could you?"

"Sure, but I don't want you harassing people."

Halliday disappeared for a couple of minutes before returning with a name. "Len Harris. He's the publican over at the Warrigal Pub."

"Thanks. There was one more thing. Were the Nolan brothers in town at the same time?"

"I'm not sure. Why?"

"They were," the young constable said. "I was on that night and as usual there was a disturbance at the pub."

"Can you remember who with?"

"Some backpackers."

"Seems to be their target of choice," Nash said.

"So you've met them?" Halliday asked.

"Let's just say that they got up close and personal with a shovel handle down in Keller Creek."

"You need to watch out for those two idiots."

"So I've been told."

"Is there anything else?"

"If I think of something I'll come see you."

Halliday nodded. "You do that."

Nash left the police station and walked out into the heat. A car drove past, its exhaust almost dragging on the ground, the roar deafening. Nash shook his head and took out his phone. He listened to the message that Gloria left for him. "Dave, you need to ring me. He's killed her. He's killed the reporter. Dammit, call me."

He redialed, still trying to process what he'd just heard. First Danny and Amy, now Maria Gallagher.

"Nash?"

"Yeah, it's me. What happened?"

"Apparently, she was tortured, too. He's coming after you, Dave. It's Betty O'Malley."

"Are you sure?"

"She as much said so. I'm headed to Perth. I—"

"No, stay away."

"I've already let the Perth police know what is happening as well as Palmer from Adelaide. This isn't good, Dave. I'm worried about you."

"I'll be fine."

"You don't know that."

"But you know me."

"Nash—"

"Stop calling me Nash, Gloria."

"I like it."

"Whatever. I have to go. I'm going to the pub."

"Be careful."

"Always."

It smelled like any other pub. Stale beer and cleaning fluids. Once upon a time the scent of stale cigarette smoke would be mixed in there somewhere.

Nash looked around the bar area. Up one end was an older man hunched over a half-glass of beer. Every town had at least one; it was like a rite of passage. There were a few others in there but for the time of day it seemed about right.

He walked up to the bar and a middle-aged waitress came down to serve him. "What'll it be, darl'?"

"Coke."

"Machine or can?"

"Can, please."

She nodded. "Can't say I blame you. The stuff that comes out of the machine tastes like diesel and cow piss."

Nash grinned. "I'm not even going to ask how you know that."

"Nor should you."

She grabbed a can from the small refrigerator behind the bar and put it on the drip mat. "Glass? Ice?"

"No, it's fine like that."

"Five bucks."

Expensive but Nash let it go. He put the money on the bar

top and said, "I'm looking for Len Harris. Is he around?"

The woman looked at Nash suspiciously. "Why might that be?"

Nash took out his ID. "Dave Nash. I'm looking for my niece."

The woman nodded and said, "I'll see if he's around."

A few minutes later, she returned with a thickset man who was wearing shorts and a collared shirt. "You Nash?"

"I am."

"Come around the end of the bar and out the back. I'll talk to you in my office."

Nash did as he was told and soon found himself inside a small, stuffy office with papers scattered everywhere. "You'll have to forgive the mess. The maid has taken the last three years off."

The former undercover shrugged. "It's paperwork."

"Isn't it. What can I do for you, Nash?"

Nash took out the picture of Tiffany and handed it over. "My niece. I was talking to Sergeant Halliday, and he said you talked to her and her boyfriend."

"That's right. I already answered a heap of bloody questions for the detectives."

"Could you help me?"

"Yeah, all right. What do you want to know?"

"They were in the pub?"

He nodded. "Yeah, they came in here asking about work. I had nothing for them."

"Halliday said they were out of money. Do you know why?"

"No."

"Did you mention this to the other police?"

"Sure. But they only seemed interested in their movements."

"How did they seem?" Nash asked.

"Actually they seemed kind of nervous. Jumpy. You know, like they were trying to get away from something."

"Any idea what?"

"No."

"Were the Nolans in here at the same time they were?" Nash asked.

Harris looked thoughtful for a time before saying, "Yes, I do believe they were. Them and Shit Head Willis."

"Is he friends with the Nolans?"

"Yeah, they all worked together for the Fisher Cannery."

"What's the Fisher Cannery?"

"Used to be a petfood place north of Meekatharra," Harris explained. "Still does it but mostly beef now. Changed over a while back but to everyone, even now, it's still the Fisher Cannery."

"All three shooters?"

"Yes. Why are you interested in them?"

"My niece and her boyfriend had trouble with them down at Keller Creek. Same happened last night with a couple of German backpackers."

"Sounds about right."

"Did you happen to be here when the others went missing?" Nash asked.

"A couple. Grace Townsend, Peggy Lester, and Franny Jensen."

"Franny Jensen?"

"Yes. Meekatharra girl. They found her a couple of days

after she disappeared."

A couple of days was way out of the pattern, but, "When was that?"

"Twenty-eighteen."

"Do you know any of the details?" Nash asked.

"Not really. You'd have to ask around up there."

"Getting back to my niece, did they say where they might go?"

"Sure, where everyone goes when they're looking for work around here."

"That is?"

"Moffat Station. Prick of a place. They work them like dogs and pay them fuck all. Not to mention the shifty shit that goes on out there."

"What sort of shifty shit?" Nash asked.

"From what I've heard there's always cattle trucks coming and going out there," Harris explained.

"I would've thought that was normal."

"A lot of it goes on at night."

"Have the police looked into it?"

"No reason to."

To Nash it sounded like the trouble he got into on his last job where cattle thieves were using stations as stopovers while shipping cattle north for live export. Obviously, it wasn't that uncommon. But if Tiffany and Rory got mixed up in it then anything could have happened.

"You sound skeptical."

"Let's just say they aren't like normal coppers."

"In what way?" Nash asked.

"That you'll have to find out for yourself. I've said too much already."

The former undercover nodded. "Tell me, the German backpackers I was telling you about, didn't come here today?"

"Might have. Wait a minute." He called out to the woman Nash had originally talked to. "Belinda! Did we have any backpackers in today?"

"Yeah."

"What did they want?"

"Moffat Station."

Harris nodded. "There's your answer."

"Are they hiring?"

The publican shrugged. "The only way to find out is ask."

Nash nodded. "Thanks."

OUTSIDE PERTH
WESTERN AUSTRALIA

A blue Ford Falcon sat on the edge of the large water-filled opencut quarry. Some one-hundred and forty feet below the surface was the bottom, littered with all kinds of debris including human remains of no less than ten people.

Joe Black looked across the Falcon at a big, tattooed man on the other side. "This better be what you say it is, Mick. I don't need this shit coming back to the surface."

Mick grinned. "There's no fucker resurfaced from down there yet, Joe. I should know, I put most of them there myself."

The man known as Mick was an enforcer for the Western Warriors motorcycle gang. Joe had called him out of the blue requesting some assistance with his current situation. Both had served together a lifetime ago. The reporter was one thing. Offing a copper was a totally different kettle of fish and he didn't want the body resurfacing.

"What did this fucker do, anyway?" Mick asked.

"Knew too much," Black replied staring at the corpse of Bruce Morrow. There was a small bullet hole at his right temple. The rest of his body bore the cuts and bruises of the vigorous interrogation he'd suffered before he died. However, Black did get the information he was searching for. They always crack in the end.

The biker shook his head. "Can't believe you did a copper."

"Is the handbrake off?"

Mick glanced down before looking back up at his friend.

CRACK!

The biker's jaw dropped as the bullet punched into his chest. "What the fuck, Joe?"

"Sorry, Mick, can't risk it."

The big man stumbled before falling to the ground. Black walked around the vehicle and stood looking down at him. The eyes, although open, were unseeing as Mick had already stopped breathing. "Shit, now I have to get you in the damned car."

A few minutes later, Black had worked up a serious sweat from the heavy exertions. Mick's dead weight had been arduous to move and had taken a herculean effort to lift him into the vehicle. Ensuring that everything was secure and ready, Black walked around behind the car and began to push it toward the pit full of water far below.

At first there was no movement, then with another large shove, the Falcon started to edge forward. It crept slowly across the gravel, crunching loudly beneath the tires, before it began to gather enough momentum to carry it over the edge to plunge into the murky depths.

Breathing heavily, Black watched the vehicle disappear beneath the water, a trail of bubbles in its wake. When the surface had resumed its glassy sheen, he turned back towards the hire car. It was time to head north.

CHAPTER TEN

**MOUNT WARRIGAL
WESTERN AUSTRALIA**

"Bruce Morrow has disappeared," Gloria informed Nash when he called her that evening. "Sometime today. No one has been able to raise him."

"Whoever that woman has sent after me certainly takes his job seriously," Nash replied.

"This isn't a joke, Nash," Gloria shot back at him.

He sighed. "Is this going to become a thing?"

"What are you talking about?"

"You calling me Nash."

"Maybe it already is."

"Fuck it, whatever."

"Have you found anything?" Gloria asked him, trying to steer the conversation in a different direction.

"Maybe. I have a hunch, actually it's more than a hunch,

that Tiffany and her boyfriend went to work out at a place called Moffat Station. Rumor has it that some very shifty stuff is going on out there. From the sound of it, the place could be used as a waystation for shipments of stolen cattle."

"Not again."

"I'm going out there tomorrow to see if they've got any work."

"That's not a good idea, Nash," Gloria cautioned him. "Not good at all."

"If I can get a job then I might be able to find out what happened to Tiffany."

"Or get yourself killed. What you need is backup. I'm coming up there tomorrow."

"I'll be fine, Gloria."

"Bullshit. Not this time. I'll get a room at the pub, and I'll be on hand if you need me."

"Is there any way of persuading you not to?"

"Not a chance in hell, buddy."

"How's our girl?" It was his turn to change the subject.

"She's fine."

There was a moment of silence.

"I miss you, Dave."

"Me, too. I'll call you tomorrow night."

"I want regular check-ins, Nash, just like when you were undercover. Understood?"

"I'll do what I can."

"Do you have a weapon?"

Nash grinned. "You bet, baby. It's dangerous, too, as you

well know."

"Asshole."

"Talk tomorrow, Gloria. Love you."

"Love you, too."

The call disconnected and Nash tossed the cell beside him on the bed. He looked at his watch. It was getting late. He could head off for a beer in the bar or just go to bed.

Suddenly he felt overwhelmingly tired. Bed was seeming like a good prospect. "Fuck it, I'll have a beer."

"How is the room?" Harris asked as he poured Nash a beer.

"The room is fine."

The publican placed Nash's beer on the bar mat and picked up the twenty dollar note sitting beside it. "I'm closing soon. If you want something else, now is the time to order it. Do you want a stubby to take back to your room?"

"No, this one will do me nicely."

Nash looked around the bar and counted a handful of patrons.

"It's always quiet this time of the week," Harris said from behind him when he noticed Nash's inspection of the place.

The former undercover nodded and took a sip of the beer. It was cold and tasted good.

"Say, did you hear the news?" Harris asked.

"What news?"

"There was a body found out in the desert late this afternoon. Place called The Bluffs. Two small plateau type hills in the middle of nowhere."

Nash stared at him. "The first I heard of it. Male or female?"

"Not sure."

The door to the bar opened and Constable Eleanor Parker walked in as though on cue. She looked tired, withdrawn. She spotted Nash and walked over to him. The look in her eyes and the expression on her face told him all he needed to know. "Tiffany?"

She gave a weird noncommittal movement of her head and said, "I'm not absolutely certain, but we think it is."

She reached into her pocket and took out a chain with a medallion on it in a plastic evidence bag. "This was taken off the body. The sergeant wanted you to have a look at it."

With a trembling hand, Nash took the bag and turned it around. It was then he saw the inscription. *To Tiffany...love mum and dad.*

Nash stared at it for a while before looking at the constable. "Can I see her?"

She shook her head. "No. It's not pretty. She's been out there a while and we're still waiting for a couple of detectives to arrive. Then there will be an exam."

He nodded. "Was she..."

The constable shook her head again. "It's too early to tell, Nash. Her body will be taken to Meekatharra where it will be examined properly. If it is her, I'm sorry for your loss."

"But we still need confirmation," he said.

"Yes, but the body ticks all the boxes."

"What about her boyfriend?"

"No sign so far."

Nash stared in silence over her shoulder at the wall. She said, "I'm sorry, Nash. I've got to go."

He looked her in the eye. "Thanks for coming to find me, Constable."

She left the bar and Nash sat down. Harris said, "I'm sorry, Nash."

"Yeah, get me another beer, will you?"

Harris moved along the bar to the taps to fill another glass. Meanwhile Nash reached for his cell. He needed to talk to Gloria.

Gloria arrived the following afternoon. She held him close, and he felt as though there was nothing else in the world that mattered other than that moment. Then, when she let him go, it all came back.

"What now?" she asked him.

"I need you to go to Meekatharra and find out about the autopsy results," he told her. "They should be doing them either late today or early tomorrow."

"But what about the other problem?" she asked. "The hitman that is coming for you. Hell, he could be here already."

"We'll worry about that if and when it happens."

"Damn it, Nash, the threat is serious."

"I know, but I need to find out what happened to Tiffany. If the events leading to her death transpired at Moffat Station, I need to find out what those were."

There was a knock on the room door.

"Yes?" Nash called out.

"It's Detective Sergeant Lee Harvey, WA Police. I'm looking for David Nash." The voice was deep, almost hollow. "I'm here with Detective Constable Roger Power."

Nash got up and was about to move when Gloria stopped him. She walked over to one of her bags and delved a hand inside, coming out with a Glock. Nash glared at her, giving her a 'What the fuck' look. She shrugged and nodded towards the door.

Nash opened the door and saw the two detectives standing in the hallway. One of them was thin, hollow-cheeked. The other, a big man whom Nash guessed was Harvey. "May we come in?" He'd been right.

Nash stepped aside and the two detectives entered. He closed the door and noticed the two men staring at Gloria. He also noticed that the Glock had magically disappeared. "This is Gloria Browning, my partner."

They nodded in her direction. Harvey said, "Yes, we've heard of Senior Constable Browning."

"What can I do for you?" Nash asked.

The big man sighed. "Consider this to be an official notification of your niece's death, Mister Nash. I'm sorry, but there is no one else."

The former undercover nodded. "So she's been positively identified?"

"No, but there isn't any mistake, it's her. A picture we have matches the remains as best we can tell. We expect DNA to seal it."

"Still, it's a bit premature, isn't it?" Nash asked.

"Maybe but I've been doing this long enough to know

when all roads lead to Rome."

"What do you know?" Gloria asked.

"We're not at liberty to say," Power piped up finally.

"Of course not."

"Were there dog bites on her legs?" Nash asked.

Harvey gave him a solemn look. "She's been out there for a while, Mister Nash. It's hard to tell."

"Yet you can tell that it's her," Nash growled.

The detective said nothing.

"Yeah, right."

"I know you're up here looking for her, Mister Nash," Harvey said. "Have you found anything out that we might need to know?"

"Not a thing."

"What was that about the dog bites?" Power asked.

"The latest victims had dog bites on their legs. You should know that. And if you did, you would also figure out that there is a possibility that the victims were being hunted."

"We're new to the investigation, Nash," Harvey said, his demeanor changing. "What are you saying about other victims? We were told that this was just a possible murder investigation, nothing about other victims."

"Fuck me," Gloria snorted. "Even Bruce Morrow knew that."

Harvey's head whipped around. "What do you know about Vic Morrow?"

"I talked to him when I was in Perth," Nash said. He walked over to his bed and picked up the folder Morrow had given him. "He gave me this."

Harvey took it and flicked through the pages before glancing up at Nash.

"Don't worry, Morrow assured me they weren't originals, and he also knew he could get into deep shit for giving it to me. But he's gone now, and he isn't coming back."

The big detective glared at Nash. "How do you know that?"

"Because there is a hitman chasing me, Detective. Sent by a fucked-up bitch called Betty O'Malley. You see, I killed her sons and now she's intent on an eye for an eye. She's already killed my brother and his wife, a reporter in Perth, and now Morrow. He's following the same trail I took. Shit, he could even be in this town by now."

Harvey looked at his partner. "This is some fucked-up shit."

Power nodded. "Just crazy enough to be true."

"We need to check this out," Harvey said, holding the folder up.

"I'll tell you what you'll be told, Detective Harvey. There is nothing to link them. It was the same thing that Morrow told me. But there is a link. The dog bites on the legs. Even the Aboriginal girl who was hit by a truck way up near Newman. The driver says he believes she was being chased by something. All I'm saying is look a little deeper and keep an open mind."

Harvey stared at Nash and nodded. "If there is something there, I'll find it."

"You can't be serious, Lee," Power growled, giving Harvey an incredulous look.

The big detective glowered back at his partner. "It won't hurt to look into it while we're up here. Are you going to hang around, Nash?"

"For a couple of days."

"I know that look. Do not interfere with the investigation,

Nash, understood?"

"Not me."

"Don't think I don't know who you are, Nash. Every copper has heard about the renegade UC who got kicked out of the force because of his attitude."

"I wasn't kicked out, Harvey, I left because I didn't suffer pricks who got up in my face."

"Well, don't get up in mine and we won't have a problem." He turned his gaze towards Gloria. "And if I were you, I'd get rid of the handgun. I'm sorry for your loss."

The two detectives left, and Gloria retrieved the Glock from its hiding spot. "Do you figure he'll look into it?"

"Maybe. But I'm not waiting to find out."

"You're going out to Moffat Station, aren't you?"

"Just as soon as the sun puts in an appearance."

A blinding ray of sunlight shone through the window, falling across Gloria as she lay partially on Nash's chest. "Ahhh, I told you, you should have closed the drapes," she said to him, putting her arm up to block the glare.

"Maybe."

Outside the pub on the street voices could be heard as guests got packed and began to leave. A car started with a roar, the hole in its exhaust doing it no favors. Reversing out of an angle park, the driver gunned the engine, and it took off along the main street, leaving deafening noise pollution in its wake.

"Nash, I've been thinking."

"What about?"

"The dead girls."

"Okay."

"What if they're not all linked?"

He shifted slightly but was pinned down by Gloria's weight. "What do you mean? The dog bites link them."

"The latter ones, yes, but not the earlier ones. Look at it, the first death was in twenty-ten, we're now in twenty-twenty-one. The first indication of the dog was when?"

"Twenty-fifteen."

"Six years seems more plausible than eleven, don't you think?"

"Maybe."

"Maybe you should focus on that part of it."

"That's what I was doing, Gloria," Nash said abruptly.

"I know, but what I'm saying is it might be easier if the timeline is shrunk down."

"Maybe."

THE GREAT NORTHERN HIGHWAY

Joe Black had left the roadhouse at Keller Creek just after midnight. The clerk there had been most helpful and given him another lead that would take him to Mount Warrigal. He intended to ask around to find out who had seen Nash, or he might be fortunate enough to discover him still there. He'd gleaned—make that tortured—one piece of interesting news from the clerk. It seemed that Nash had had a run in with some local kangaroo shooters and he'd put them both down.

Black kept driving north, the monotony of white lines passing beneath his tires his only company for a while. At least ten minutes later, a set of headlights in the rearview mirror told him he was no longer alone. Even though a long way off he could tell that they were dazzlingly bright. More than two, perhaps four.

Black reached across to the passenger seat and picked up the handgun, a Glock 19, and placed it on his lap.

Keeping his speed steady, it didn't take long before the interior of his ride was illuminated by the blinding lights of a 4X4 that raced up behind him.

The sound of a horn blared out across the night, then the vehicle surged forward, its alloy bull-bar nudging the rear of Black's vehicle. It then backed off momentarily before repeating the maneuver.

Black muttered a curse and sped up, glancing down at the speedometer which revealed he was now sitting on one-twenty. Hit a kangaroo at that speed, especially a big bastard, and shit was all over. So, Black eased the pressure on the gas pedal.

Not hurriedly, just put his foot on the brake and depressed it slightly so the vehicle he drove slowed gradually until it rolled to a halt.

The 4X4 came to a stop behind him but left its lights on full beam. Yahooing could be heard emanating from the cabin, but Black remained unmoving in his vehicle, waiting.

Squinting against the glare of the spotlights, he watched in his outside mirror as the driver of the 4X4 opened his door and dropped to the asphalt, the interior light revealing two of them. The driver stepped around the open door and called out, "Hey, you all right in there?"

When no answer came, he called out, "We was just having some fun. No harm."

Black undid his seatbelt then reached for the door latch, pulling it back to release the catch, then pushed the door fully open. He swung his legs out and rose from the seat, unfolding his body as he stood up, keeping the Glock out of sight.

"Hey, Pete, he looks cross. Ha-ha."

Black kept walking, squinting against the glare of the lights.

"I wouldn't come any closer if I were you, mate," Jimmy called out in warning.

But Black was in no mood to be taking advice from anyone let alone these bogans. Instead, he brought up the Glock he had hidden and started firing. He didn't stop until both the Nolan brothers were dead.

Sergeant Ben Davis slowed his Land Cruiser to a stop and stared through the bug splattered windshield at the burned-out hulk on the side of the highway. He could identify it immediately by the frame on the rear. Jimmy and Pete Nolan's rig.

Reaching for his computer console, he typed in the details of the stop, giving a quick scan of the area to check for threats or any details he might have missed. He climbed out and walked slowly forward. The area immediately surrounding the vehicle was blackened and some of the grass and stunted shrubs also were burned. But with no wind the previous night the red desert had acted as a fire break and kept the flames trapped in the vicinity.

As he approached the vehicle something caught his eye on the asphalt. He stared at it. A pool of almost black, barely moist but drying fast under the already hot sun. Blood. Davis had seen it enough times to know what it was.

He immediately drew his sidearm, darting his eyes around the location before finally stepping forward.

He could smell the sickly-sweet scent of burnt flesh well before he saw them. Having encountered it only once before, it was something he had no desire to repeat; he would never forget it. Stopping level with the driver's door, he glanced around the area once more, taking in the flat and arid red dirt terrain with no other signs of life. Bringing his eyes back to the burned-out vehicle before him, he looked into the cabin, the window no longer there. Two bodies, charred beyond recognition had assumed a bizarre rictus in death. As he took in as many details as possible he noticed them. The two holes in the door itself. Bullet holes.

He was definitely looking at a double homicide.

CHAPTER ELEVEN

MOFFAT STATION
WESTERN AUSTRALIA

Nash moved the Commodore over onto the shoulder to allow a B-triple road train carting cattle more room to get past on the narrow road leading to the Moffat Station homestead. He glanced at the truck itself. The name on the side said, Cowral Cattle Cartage.

It rattled past and Nash could smell the cattle manure dripping from the crates. Then it was gone, leaving behind a pall of dust hanging in the air, drifting to the west on the slight morning breeze.

The Commodore's front left tire hit a pothole and the resulting shudder rattled Nash's teeth. "Shit," he hissed as he felt pain shoot through his mouth as he bit his tongue. He tasted blood as the sharp pain turned to an annoying throb.

For the next ten kilometers the road twisted and turned,

crossing numerous dry creek beds and navigating a couple of jump ups. Then as the Commodore topped a low ridge the homestead appeared before him, an island of green surrounded by a sea of red and stunted scrub.

When Nash pulled up outside the house yard he sat in the Commodore for a short time before climbing out. He counted four hands walking around looking busy, but none even gave him a second glance.

"Who are you and what do you want?" a voice from behind him asked.

Nash turned to see a man walking towards him dressed in jeans, long-sleeved shirt, and a cowboy hat. "I'm looking for some work."

"Oh, yeah?" the man said skeptically.

"That's right. Bloke at the pub said you lot were always hiring."

"Not today, we're not."

Nash made a point of looking around. "Seems to me everyone is pretty busy."

"What's your name?"

"Ray Nash." Going in without the proper planning was dangerous which was why Nash decided to use his last name. People you worked with usually made a habit of calling you by your last name. Less chance of mistakes that way.

"I'm Olsen, station foreman. And like I said, we haven't—"

"What's wrong, Olsen?" a man called out from near a large machinery shed.

"City slicker looking for some work, Mister Moffat."

"Fine, put him to work with the other useless lot."

"I told him we've got nothing."

"Now why would you do that? There's plenty to do now that we have other things to tend to. When you're done there, head out to the back sixty and check on the cattle out there. We're shipping them in a few days."

"Yes, sir."

Nash grinned at Olsen. "Where do I put my car?"

Olsen glared at him. "Put it out the back of the machinery shed. Then come with me."

Nash parked the Commodore and climbed out. He took out a cap, locked it up and was about to walk back around the shed when he caught sight of Werner. He walked over to the German who was rolling up some fencing wire. "Werner, hi."

Werner looked at Nash and seemed surprised to see him. "Dave?"

Shit. "No, call me Ray or Nash."

Werner frowned. "Why?"

"Because I'm hiding from someone and I don't want anyone to know who I really am," Nash lied.

"All right."

"Please, I really need you to keep it a secret, okay?"

"Sure."

"You'll tell Emma?"

"Yes."

"Thanks. I have to go. I'll see you tonight."

"Bye."

Although it was his first hiccup, he hoped that it would

be his last. That was, if Werner or Emma didn't bugger it up.

He walked back around and found Olsen waiting for him in a battered Nissan Patrol, tray back. Nash climbed in.

"What fucking took you so long?"

"I got lost."

"Smartass."

Olsen started the Nissan and shoved it into gear. The wheels spun as he put his foot down and it wasn't long before a cloud of dust was following them along a track leading west.

After ten minutes of traveling in silence, Olsen pulled over near a trough and bore. They both climbed out and Olsen said, "Check that ballcock."

"The what?" Nash asked, feigning ignorance.

"Shit. The part where the water comes out. Make sure that it's working properly."

Nash went over to the trough and bent over where the ballcock was. The trough was full of water and the valve seemed to be working fine. He stood up and turned just in time for Olsen's fist to crash into his jaw.

Nash reeled away, stars flashing inside his head. He staggered before going down to his knees, hunched over as he tried to clear his vision. Shaking his head, he looked up just as Olsen sank a boot into his stomach. The former undercover lurched to the side and rolled over onto his back, his knees now drawn up to his chest.

Nash let out a groan. Pain shot through his body. He looked up as Olsen loomed over him. "Just remember who's in fucking charge around here, mate. Consider this your first and only warning, any trouble out of you and I'll fucking kill you."

Nash's face was red as he gasped for breath. He looked up at Olsen and nodded slightly. "Sure, whatever you say."

"Now you can walk back to the homestead."

As Nash lay there, he heard Olsen's boots crunching on dirt and gravel as he walked back to the 4X4. The door slammed and the motor wound over before roaring to life. He heard the grate of gears as the foreman put it into first, and then the roar of acceleration as it drove away.

Nash climbed to his feet and stood watching the cloud of dust lowering as more distance was put between them as the vehicle raced towards the homestead. "Guess I'll be putting you at the top of my list, asshole."

He then turned back to the water trough to have a drink. He looked at the green hanging from the sides and scrunched his face into a grimace before cupping his hands in the water and lifting them to his lips. He sipped tentatively before scooping more water and taking a deeper draught, resigned to the fact that it could be his last for a while as he faced the long, dry walk back to the homestead.

It was late afternoon when Nash arrived back at the headquarters. He wandered into the yard and found that the hands' presence had almost doubled. It was getting close to dark, which meant it was nearing knock off time.

"You look like shit," said a young hand as he walked up to Nash. "What happened?"

"Olsen."

"Say no more. The guy can be a fucking prick at times. It's just about knock off time anyway. How about I shout you a beer once we're done. By the way, the name is Terry Smith."

"Ray Nash."

"Pleased to meet you, Ray," Smith said, offering Nash his hand.

Nash took it. Smith's grip was firm, the callouses digging into Nash's palm. "You, too."

"Stuff it, come with me. I'll show you where to put your shit."

"I just have to get it out of the car."

"Fine. I'll meet you in the machinery shed."

There was a roar as the Nissan came back into their yard with Olsen behind the wheel. He brought the vehicle to a stop in a cloud of dust and climbed out. He looked over at Nash, a smirk on his face. "Have a good walk?"

Nash ignored him and turned away, heading towards the machinery shed with the Commodore parked behind it.

He leaned in to get his gear out, which was all packed into a bag, then came back around to the front where he met Smith.

Smith took him over to the station-hand quarters. It was one big, long building, split up into separate rooms, each room able to sleep four men or women. "We all sleep in here," he said. "There's a couple of spare bunks in with me. You'll be right in there."

Inside the air was hot, almost stifling. Nash put his bag on the floor beside his bed and sat down on the mattress.

"Do you have a swag or something, Nash?" Smith asked.

"No, nothing like that."

"Sleeping bag?"

"No."

"Guess we'll have to find you something then."

Smith went to a small bar fridge and opened it. A quick glance through the man's legs told Nash that it was well stocked with beer. Smith tore the plastic wrapping on a six-pack and pulled two bottles from it and passed one to the former undercover, closing the fridge door with his boot. "Wrap your lips around that. It'll wash the dust away."

Nash took the top off and placed the cold bottle onto his forehead, enjoying the icy moisture which formed a muddy smear in the dust before forming a drip that fell from his eyebrow. He pulled it away and took a long pull. After he'd swallowed, he looked at the label on the bottle before casually saying, "Tell me about Olsen?"

"You already know what there is to know. The bloke is a fucking prick."

"How long have you been here?"

Smith had a drink of his beer, swallowed, and then said, "Four months. Give or take a few days."

"So not long then?"

"Not in the scheme of things."

"When I was talking to the feller at the pub in town, he said that people come and go a lot of the time here. What's the story with that? Is the guy a bastard to work for?"

"You ask a lot of questions for a new bloke."

"Just wanting to know what I've got myself in for."

Smith nodded. "All right, I'll give you the short story. The boss is a prick to work for, the foreman is a bastard, and the days are long and hot. People come and go all the time because they can't hack the work. They have a permanent workforce here of seven. The rest is made up of backpackers and people like that who come out here thinking they can do the work and then find out in a hurry that they can't."

"Are you permanent workforce?"

"Ask me again in another six months. If I'm still here, then yeah, I guess I am."

"Why wouldn't you be?" Nash asked.

"How about you tell me about you?" Smith said changing the direction of the conversation.

"Ray Nash. Sick of the busy life, looking for a change. Wife left me for another guy, took the kid with her. Figured I'd come out here and see if I could forget all my troubles."

"Takes a hard guy to stick it out here, Nash. It's a hard country. You hard enough?"

Nash had another drink of his beer. "I guess we'll find out, hey."

"I guess we will."

"I passed the cattle truck on the way in. Do they ship out many?"

"It's a big station, trucks come and go all the time."

Nash smiled innocently. "Bit like the backpackers, huh?"

"Yeah, something like that."

"Where are you from, Smith?" Nash asked.

"Condamine, Queensland. My parents used to own a property there. That was until the drought forced them off. That and the bank. They lost everything."

"How did you end up over here?"

"Hit the road looking for work. Never stopped till I reached northwestern Australia. What about you?"

"Me? Searching for something I still haven't found."

"Aren't we all? Shit, I'm going for a shower before all these dicks use the hot water."

"Where do we do that?" Nash asked.

"End of the building. There are two showers."

"Fine, I'll be along shortly."

"Don't be too long," Smith said. "Like I said, the hot water don't last too long."

After the hand had disappeared, Nash took out his cell and called Gloria.

"I was wondering when you'd call," she said. "How is it going?"

"I'm in. Already made a couple of friends."

He quickly told her about Olsen.

She came back with, "That's what I love about you. You play so well with others. Do you still have the Glock?"

"Check in your bag."

"Fuck, Nash, I told you to take it," Gloria growled.

"Couldn't take the risk. What about you?"

"I'm going to see if I can get some results tomorrow."

"OK. Good luck with that. Listen, I have to go. Love you."

"Love you, too. Be careful, Nash."

"You know me."

"I do." Her voice was grim. "Promise not to kill too many people."

"I'll try."

He'd just disconnected the call when Smith came back into their room. "What happened to you?"

Nash patted the mattress he was sitting on. "Couldn't be stuffed hauling my sorry ass off the bed."

"If you move fast there's a spare shower."

Climbing to his feet, Nash said, "I'd better get moving then."

Surprisingly, the showers were relatively clean; even better, the water still hot and Nash let it cascade down over his body trying to have it wash away the aches from the long walk over the rugged ground back to the station.

Once he was done, he dried off and headed back to the room he shared with Smith who was out on the veranda that ran the length of the accommodation block, drinking a beer. From inside the other rooms, he could hear voices and laughter.

The sun was well and truly down now, and the stars were up. Nash went inside and right away knew that someone had gone through his stuff. He turned his head and looked out the open door of the room he shared with Smith, wondering if his new roommate was a plant or a thief. He decided to let it go but would now keep a closer eye on the young man.

Nash grabbed another beer and went outside. "Starting to

cool off," he noted.

"Does that out here," Smith said.

Suddenly the sound of a revving engine could be heard, and headlights danced on the horizon. "Shit, here we go," Smith groaned.

Olsen appeared out of the darkness. "Smith, get your ass moving. Tell the others to come over to the yard."

Olsen glared at Nash before walking away. "Fuck, I was all clean too," Smith growled.

"I'll come and help," Nash said.

The hand shook his head. "No, mate, this one's for the regulars only."

"You sure?"

"Yeah. You show up and Olsen will have a fucking foal."

Nash held up both hands. "That's fine, I'll just enjoy this beer."

"Half your luck," Smith said and turned to walk along the veranda, stopping at two doorways. His arrival was greeted with a string of curses before the other 'regular' hands appeared and they all headed towards the stockyards.

The truck arrived and maneuvered into place. Nash could hear bellowing cattle coming from the stock crates.

Movement beside him drew his attention as Werner appeared. "What is happening?"

"Load of cattle coming in," Nash replied.

"Should we go and help?"

"No, I was told not to."

The German gave a grunt and nodded.

"Listen, did you have that talk to Emma?"

He nodded. "Yes."

"How are you faring after the other night?"

"Getting better."

"Good."

Nash put the beer down and got to his feet. He stepped down off the veranda and Werner asked, "Where are you going?"

"It's better you don't know."

Using the shadows, Nash circled around towards the yards. Once he figured he had gone far enough he stood beside a tractor and watched the men work.

Two trailers were being unloaded, the cattle filling the yards. Over the bawling sound, Nash heard Moffat's voice, "Olsen, once we're done here, take them out to the north paddock. They can stay there for a week before they get shifted again."

"Got it, Boss. Smith, Webster, Groves, that's your job."

Nash remained observing for a few more minutes then went back to the station hands' quarters. He ran through a few scenarios in his head.

Stolen cattle coming in before being shipped out. Could be as innocent as a truckload coming in for the station but why ship them out so soon?

Nash dug into his pocket for his cell and dialed Gloria.

"That was quick."

"I need you to dig into Moffat for me."

"OK, what's his first name?"

Nash paused. "I have no idea."

She sighed. "I'll find out."

"And his foreman, Olsen."

"First or last name?" Gloria asked.

"Last."

"First name?"

"No idea."

"Shit, Nash."

"I have one more name. Terry Smith. Young bloke, says he comes from Condamine."

"Anything else?"

"No, that about covers it."

"Man, you're lucky you have me," Gloria said.

"Don't I know it." He grinned to himself.

With the call complete there was nothing else to do except go to bed. Then as he drifted off to sleep, he suddenly realized he'd had nothing to eat.

"Get up if you're hungry," Smith said as he kicked the bottom on the bed Nash was sleeping in. "Grub will be ready shortly."

"What time did you get to bed?" Nash asked.

"Sometime tonight."

Nash nodded and sat up rubbing his face then swung his legs over the side before standing. He looked outside through the curtainless window. The sun was just breaking above the horizon. "What time is it?"

"About five."

Nash got dressed and pulled his boots on. "Where do we eat?"

"We have a place with a barbecue and a roof over it. Kind of like a camp kitchen. The cook sets up there of a morning and night so we can eat. The trick is to get there before the sun is fully up or you'll be eating flies with your bacon."

"Lead the way."

Everyone was there including Moffat and Olsen. They sat around eating their breakfast while the chorus of early morning sounds, cows, crows, galahs, and numerous other animals ushered in another day of dust, flies, and heat.

Nash sat away from Werner and Emma to lessen the risk of something happening. There were, however, quite a few backpackers working for Moffat.

Once breakfast was done with, the workers were assigned their jobs. Olsen looked at Nash. "Can you read a map?"

"Yes."

"Good. You'll be out checking fences and a couple of troughs. They're all marked on the map so if you can read the map you should be right. Take a sat phone with you just in case anything happens."

Nash nodded. "On my own?"

"That's right. Do you need someone to hold your hand?"

A couple of the hands chuckled.

"You offering?" Nash shot back at him.

Olsen glared at him and said, "You should be back by midafternoon. If you're not, then I'll want to know why. And take plenty of water with you."

"Yes, sir."

As breakfast broke up, Smith came over to Nash. "Come with me and I'll set you up with a vehicle."

He followed Smith around to the machinery shed where the station mechanic was working on a Toyota Land Cruiser tray back. "Jacko, you finished with this thing?"

The curly-haired mechanic stuck his head up. "Just tightening up the last nut. You want it, Smithy?"

"No, Nash here needs some wheels to do some fences and troughs."

Jacko closed the hood, looked at Nash, and said, "It's all yours."

Nash backed it out of the shed and took it over to the fuel bowser to fill it up. Smith brought him over a four-liter container of water. "There you go. Get stuck out there without anything to drink and you're fucked."

Nash put it in the cab and was about to climb in when he noticed one of the hands following Emma in a way he found troubling. "Smithy, who is that over there?"

"Emma? She's from Germany. She—"

"No, the bloke following her?"

"Knackers Ellis. He's—where are you going?"

Nash had a feeling something was wrong and started following the pair. They disappeared behind one of the sheds.

"Hey, Nash, what the fuck?" Getting no response, Smith followed him.

Nash found them when he turned the corner of the shed. Ellis had Emma pressed against the shed, his jeans undone and half down around his thighs. He turned her around and pulled her jeans down far enough to get access.

Then Nash suddenly realized something. She wasn't fighting it. She was letting it happen, encouraging it.

Oblivious to his presence, they kept going so Nash backed around the corner, turning into Smith.

"What's going on, Nash?"

"I thought she was in trouble."

Smith shook his head. "They've been doing it since she got here."

"What about her friend?"

"He either knows and says nothing or is too dumb to realize. However, it isn't none of my business. Come on, you still need a rifle."

"Cows going to shoot me?"

"Dogs. Been a few getting around."

"Fine."

CHAPTER TWELVE

MEEKATHARRA
WESTERN AUSTRALIA

The autopsy had been done at the local hospital by the only man there qualified to do so. Doctor Rick Hunter had been performing them for the past six years and was becoming tired of the task, looking to move on.

He glanced up from his desk when Gloria was shown in and gave her a tired smile. "Mrs. Browning?"

"Miss Browning. Or Senior Constable if you prefer?"

"A police officer? Are you newly posted here?"

She shook her head. "No, I'm from Emerald in Queensland. I'm in Western Australia with my partner, Dave Nash."

"What can—" he stopped. "Nash? He's not…"

"Uncle," Gloria replied, knowing what he was about to say.

"I'm sorry for your loss."

"Can you tell me anything at all about how Tiffany died?"

Hunter hesitated. "I probably shouldn't but since you're police, maybe it won't hurt. I can trust your discretion?"

"Of course."

"She was shot from behind."

Gloria nodded. "Any idea how long she was deceased before being found?"

"A week maybe."

Gloria frowned. "That means she was kept alive for a while before she was killed."

"That would be my judgement."

"Doctor, was there any sign of bite marks on her legs?"

"Bite marks? Nothing human."

"I'm not talking human. I'm talking dog."

"Of course, there are dingoes out there everywhere."

"I'm not talking about ones that tried to eat her. I'm talking about bite marks around the legs, any that could be classed as defensive."

Hunter frowned, suddenly his weary attitude had disappeared. "What is this all about?"

"Before Tiffany was found, Dave was looking for her. He did some investigating and came up with a linking factor on at least three girls that were found. All had dog bites on their legs as though they were being hunted."

The doctor was frozen for a moment as he tried to process what Gloria was saying. "I'm not sure I understand."

Gloria passed him a list of names. "Could you look at these for me?"

He took the paper and studied it for a while before looking up at Gloria. "Oh, dear."

Gloria watched patiently as he studied his own paperwork. "How—how could I have missed this? All together I see what you are saying but you have to understand, they come in one at a time with such a time gap between them, I—"

"That doesn't matter," Gloria assured him. "The detectives should have picked it up."

"Looking at the reports I think you might be right. There could well be a definition from the bite marks. Especially the ones on the legs."

"So they could have been chased by dogs?"

"Yes."

"You said that Tiffany was shot. Did you find a bullet?"

Hunter shook his head. "No, it passed through her. I don't know if the police found one. All I can say that it would have been a high-powered rifle."

"Like hunters would use?"

"Yes."

The door opened and two familiar people walked through the opening. "Well, well, what do we have here?"

The detectives had arrived.

"I hope you aren't trying to interfere with an ongoing investigation, Senior Constable?" Harvey asked.

"Not me, Detective," Gloria replied. "I was just leaving."

"I think that would be best."

As she made to leave, Harvey stopped her. "There was one thing that you may like to know. Yesterday morning two kangaroo shooters were found in their burned-out wreck north of Keller Creek. We're certain they had been shot before being incinerated. Preceding that a clerk at the Keller Creek Roadhouse had been tortured and killed within hours of the second incident. It has caused us to bring in more detectives than we would like and shut down the highway between Keller Creek and Mount Warrigal. However, my point is that from their initial investigations your Mister Nash—"

"Has had contact with both of them?"

"Yes."

"Do they think it could be him?"

"If you mean your mysterious hitman then all I will say is that they are looking into it."

"If he has made it that far then he could be in Mount Warrigal," Gloria pointed out.

It was Power who spoke this time. "We have the Mount Warrigal police keeping an eye out for strangers in town."

Gloria nodded.

"By the way, where is your other half?" Harvey asked.

"I'm not quite sure."

MOFFAT STATION
WESTERN AUSTRALIA

The heat inside the 4X4 was stifling. No air-conditioning meant driving with the windows down and the flies and dust becoming more than just a nuisance.

The route marked on the map took him east. Each trough he checked was fine and the fences were, too. Then he noted that his route would take him back around to the north.

After a couple more troughs and a kilometer of fence line he saw the cattle in the distance. Nash stopped the Land Cruiser and stared at them through the shimmering heat haze which made the landscape appear waterlogged.

His thought processes took him back to the night before and the newly-arrived cattle he had seen come in and he wondered if they were the same ones. *I guess there's only one way to find out.*

Nash put the Land Cruiser in gear and turned the wheel as it moved forward. It bumped over the rough terrain until he pulled it to a stop. The cattle looked at him for a moment before going back to foraging for food.

Nash drove forward slowly in amongst the cattle. He stopped again and took out his cell. Waiting for a heifer to move around slightly he was in a better position to take a picture of the brand. Looking around he noticed that the brands all appeared to be the same. But then he saw one which stood out as different. The camera on the cell went to work again.

It was true that they could have been bought legitimately but running the brands would also find if they had been stolen.

He tried to send the pictures to Gloria but there wasn't any signal. He'd have to do it when he got back.

Suddenly Nash noticed the dust cloud coming towards where he was. At its base he could see the 4X4. He was sure that whoever it was could see him, so he sat there and opened his bottle of water.

The vehicle came on and swung around to stop beside him so both drivers were looking at each other. A familiar face glared at him. "What the fuck are you doing here, Nash?" Olsen growled.

Nash held up the water bottle. "Taking a drink break. Damn hot out here if you hadn't noticed."

"Stay away from the cattle," the foreman warned him. "There's no reason to be here with them. Especially when you know fuck all about them."

Nash made a show of screwing the lid on the bottle. "All right, I'll remember that."

"What have the fences and troughs been like?"

"So far, so good."

Olsen nodded. He pointed across the hood of the Land Cruiser. "See those escarpments over there?"

Nash turned his head and looked through the dirty windshield. In the distance he could see the orange faces of the escarpments topped with the green of a smattering of stunted trees. "Yes."

"At the base of them is a large rock pool. Head over there and have a look. Make sure it has water in it. If it doesn't, let me know."

Nash nodded. "OK."

Olsen started the vehicle he was in and called out, "And stay away from the cattle."

Nash waved as he disappeared, leaving behind him a cloud of dust. As Nash started his own vehicle he wondered if he'd gotten away with it.

The waterhole was there, alright. At the base of an orange-faced cliff surrounded by sand and eucalypts. Nash got out of the vehicle and walked closer to the billabong. The water within it seemed to be black in color, most probably from the sediment from the rock wall.

Nash stared at it in amazement. Australia was certainly a country of wondrous and diverse landscapes. He walked to the water's edge. All around he could see dog tracks mixed in with those of cattle. Also kangaroo which indicated the waterhole was well utilized by the wildlife.

A black cockatoo squawked from high above in one of the eucalypts as it protested the intrusion of the human. Beside it sat another and both were soon voicing their noisy opinions about Nash's presence.

He turned to walk back to the Land Cruiser when movement caught his eye to the west of the waterhole. Maybe a hundred or so meters from where he stood. He narrowed his eyes against the harsh glare of the sun and saw that it was a dog. A dingo maybe but it was carrying something in its mouth.

Nash frowned as curiosity started to get the better of him. He walked back to the Land Cruiser and took out the rifle. It was a Remington .243 caliber bolt action complete with scope.

He worked the bolt and put a round in the breech. Then Nash brought it up to his shoulder and pointed the weapon towards the retreating dingo. He tucked his eye in behind the scope and peered through.

It was indeed a dingo, and it was carrying something long and thick. Nash didn't know why but he squeezed the trigger of the rifle and it slammed back into his shoulder as it fired.

A puff of red-orange dirt erupted out in front of the animal, and it dropped what it had been carrying before skittering off to the right into some scrub.

But the dingo wasn't the only animal disturbed by the shot. The whiplash of the rifle cleared the two Black Cockatoos from their perch, and numerous other parrots and a couple of galahs.

Nash walked towards the area where the dingo had dropped its load. As he covered the distance, his boots kicked up small puffs of fine dust and crunched on the gravelly ground.

When he got within ten feet of the object he stopped. He stared at it for a long time before he realized what it was. Long, thick, with a hand missing some fingers at the end.

"Shit a fucking brick," Nash hissed. He stared at it for a long time before walking up to it. "What the fuck have I found?"

He turned his head in the direction the dingo had come from. There was a clump of ironstone rocks which Nash assumed was where the animal had been. He glanced at the arm again and started trudging towards the rocks, his dread growing with each step.

Then he saw it, turned his head, and threw up in the dirt at his feet.

How long the body had been there, Nash had no idea. But the elements and scavengers had certainly made a good mess of it. He knew he shouldn't touch anything, but Nash needed to see if he could find anything which might identify who it was before the place started to crawl with police.

As he poked about the remains the only thing that caught his attention was a necklace. Tarnished by time and bodily fluids, it still stood out to him. Nash reached down and pulled it free. The medallion hanging from it was flat and round. On it was engraved a picture of an angel. Nash turned it over. There was something engraved on the back as well, but he couldn't quite make out what.

He spat on it and rubbed it clean. Now he could clearly see it. The inscription read: *Love from Tiffy.*

Nash bowed his head. He was pretty sure he'd just found Rory Williams.

Moffat stared at Nash. "Go back to the homestead. We'll take care of this."

Olsen nodded. "Don't say anything about it to anyone. Understood?"

"What about notifying the police?" Nash asked.

It was a question any normal person would ask.

"They're on their way," Moffat said. "I called them before

I left."

Nash knew it was a lie. The last thing they wanted was for police and detectives nosing around if they were using the station as a transit route for stolen stock. But at the minute there was nothing he could do about it. He reached into his pocket and touched the necklace. "I'll see you back there then."

"Remember, not a word until the police have investigated," Olsen reminded him. "We don't want stories getting around. People won't want to work out here anymore."

Nash climbed into the Land Cruiser and started back to the homestead. He glanced in the rearview mirror and through the swirling dust thought he saw Olsen take out a shovel from the tray of the other vehicle.

CHAPTER THIRTEEN

MOFFAT STATION
WESTERN AUSTRALIA

"I'm worried, Nash," Gloria said after he told her the story. "There seems to be a dark shadow hanging over that place."

"What worries me more," said Nash, "is that Tiffany's body was found twenty kilometers from here."

"What are you thinking?" Gloria asked.

"I don't know but the boss and foreman here were keen to cover up the death. I'm reasonably sure that they are using this place as a transit station."

"Are you alright?"

"I'm fine. Just concentrating on getting to the bottom of it before I think too much about the other."

"This is like some movie, Nash. Bodies are piling up everywhere."

"What do you mean?"

She told him about the shooters and the clerk. "They seem to think it could be the hitman."

"Stay in Meekatharra for a while, Gloria," he warned her. "Mount Warrigal isn't safe for you."

"All right."

"What did you find out today?"

She told him what the doctor had said and how he'd failed to connect the others. "That was when the detectives showed up."

"Anything else?"

"I ran down the names you gave me. I'll start with Doug Moffat. No priors, not married. Was but his wife left him eight years back. The station was up to its ears in debt until a few years ago when payments started to flow regularly."

"Probably when the shipments of stolen cattle started to come through," Nash said.

"The interesting part is that Lionel Olsen started working at the station around the same time."

"Where does he come from?" Nash asked.

"Meekatharra. He has an uncle who operates a meat works northwest of there. Does petfood as well."

This gave Nash another reason for pause. He'd already heard about it from the publican. Then he said, "Dig into it and the livestock ports up this way."

"You looking to see if any of them had any uptick in shipments?"

"Something like that."

"Already checked. There was none," Gloria told him.

"Then that leaves the meat works."

"I'll scrutinize it shortly."

"Next, I have some brands for you."

"Fire away."

"A, D, nine, and B, 2, three."

"Written down," Gloria said.

"Did you get anything on Terry Smith?"

"Smith is the oldest alias in the book," Gloria informed him. "No Terry Smith from Condamine in Queensland. However, there was a Terry Wells. He has outstanding fines and warrants. One of which for assault. Put a police officer in hospital when he was arrested for disturbing the peace. Ran before his court date."

"Do you have a picture?" Nash asked.

"I'll send you one when we've finished here. Do you think that Tiffany and Rory discovered what was going on?"

"I don't know. But Rory died here, and Tiffany was found a fair way away. If they died around the same time—"

"No," Gloria said cutting him off. "The doctor said she was killed a week before she was found."

"Rory has been dead longer than that."

"Are you sure?"

"I'm not a doctor but yeah, I'm sure," Nash said.

"This is getting worse, Dave," Gloria said.

He noted her use of his Christian name. She was right of course. There was a hitman behind them somewhere. There was a serial killer out there in the Western Australian wilderness, and an organized cattle-stealing ring right under his feet. He had a feeling that things were only going to get worse. "Just see what you can find out about the meat works and the brands. I'll try and track what happened to Rory and Tiffany from here."

"Be careful, Dave."

"Tell our little girl daddy loves her."

"I will."

He disconnected the cell just in time because Smith suddenly appeared around the corner of the hay shed where he'd been making the call to Gloria. "There you are. I've been looking for you everywhere. We got the good end of the stick for once."

Nash stared at the grinning face. "What do you mean?"

"We have to go to town to get some things. Because it is late, we'll stay there and come back tomorrow."

"By town you mean…"

"Mount Warrigal."

"Of course, you do."

MOUNT WARRIGAL
WESTERN AUSTRALIA

"This one will do," Nash said pointing out the Railway Hotel. "Pull in here."

"You sure you don't want to stay at the Warrigal?" Smith asked.

"Is there something wrong with this one?"

"No. I'm easy," Smith replied as he pulled the Land Cruiser

over into the angle carpark between an old Ford Falcon and a green Holden Commodore. He turned it off and climbed out.

Nash followed suit. "Beer first?"

"Shit, yes," Smith replied. "It's not often that we get to town. I plan on having a beer and a big steak."

"Sounds good," Nash agreed.

When they went inside, the bar had only a few patrons sitting nursing drinks. Which was to be expected for the middle of the week. They ordered their beers and while at the bar, Smith told the waitress that they were looking for a couple of rooms as well.

"No problem," she replied with a smile.

"Thanks, Gail. Any chance of a couple of steaks as well?"

"Sure."

They found a table and sat down. Nash looked around the bar and saw that most of the tables were indeed empty. There were a couple of old timers playing eight ball and a few more at the bar.

"Do you know why the boss and Olsen took off today?" Smith asked.

Nash shook his head. "No."

The hand left it go at that.

They had another beer while waiting for their food and talked about different things. Their meals came and went, and Nash had to agree that it wasn't half bad. One more beer and things were starting to relax.

"What are you doing out here, Nash?" Smith asked. "You don't seem to fit."

Nash stared at him for a moment as though he was trying to decide whether or not to tell him. "Got into some trouble in Melbourne."

Smith grunted. "Sounds familiar."

"You, too?"

"Yeah. Fucking stupid really. But I can't go back."

"Me neither. The copper I hit is an asshole."

"Shit, you made that mistake, too?"

Nash gave him a fake look of surprise. "Don't tell me."

"The copper at Condamine was a prick," Smith explained. "Tried to lock me up for being drunk. Roughed me around a bit until I couldn't take anymore. Then I lashed out. Once was all it took. I put him in the hospital. That was the end. He told them that I picked something up and hit him from behind. How do you get a broken nose when you're hit from behind? When he fell, he hit the back of his head, but he managed to get the doctor who examined him to say it was the other way around."

Nash could tell that he was speaking the truth. Could see it in his eyes. "And now you're here."

"Out of the frying pan and into the fire," he muttered.

"Can't be that bad."

"Yeah. What about you?"

"Crooked cop tried to stitch me up on a theft charge," Nash lied. "I had to run. Reached out to my brother who told me his daughter was up this way working on a station. I was going to meet her there, but it looks like she's gone."

"What station?" Smith asked.

"Moffat."

Nash waited for a reaction, but one never came. Instead, Smith asked, "What was her name?"

"Tiffany Nash."

"No, not heard of her." But his eyes lied.

"She was traveling with her boyfriend, Rory."

"No." Another lie. Suddenly he said, "I'm tired. Might turn in."

Nash nodded. "Me, too."

"Hey, babe," Nash said.

"Nash, twice in one day. What's up? Are you alright?"

"I'm fine. I'm back in Mount Warrigal."

"Oh, no. Why?"

"Have to pick up stuff for the station. I'm here with our friend Mister Smith."

"How is that going?" Gloria asked.

"It's amazing how loose a tongue will get after a couple of beers," he explained. "He spilled about what happened back in Condamine."

Nash went on to tell her about what was said and more. "Are you sure he's lying?"

"Yes, almost certain. I think he figures he's in too deep at this place and can't see a way out. I'll give it a day or so and see what else I can get. How did you go?"

"It's all coming together," she explained. "I checked out those brands. One was registered to a Walters Trading Inc. in South Australia and the other to the Barnes Stock company in

New South Wales. I reached out to a friend at Rural Crimes in New South Wales, and she confirmed that there has been some stock go missing within the past fortnight there."

"What about the meat works?"

"Owned by a man named Byron Willis," Gloria explained. "It used to be a petfood slaughterhouse. Kangaroos, mostly. But then a few years back it changed. From what I could see there was a lot of money spent to convert it to beef."

"Money that he didn't have?" Nash asked.

"According to my contact in financial crimes who did some digging, the money came from an outside source."

"So he runs the show for a much bigger…syndicate maybe?"

"It's possible."

"What else did you find out?"

"Nothing more."

Nash sighed. "So we can assume that this is where the stolen cattle end up. For an operation like that they would need to have a few others in the pot. DPI, trucking company, and others."

"Yes, but if it is making a lot of money, then it's not showing it. It's barely making a profit."

"What about workers?" Nash asked. "Do you think they might know if something shifty is going on?"

"They wouldn't know any better," Gloria said. "Do workers in ordinary meat works know if they are killing legally bought animals? I doubt it. All you would have to do is pay taxes and forge the books. To someone on the outside it all looks legitimate. The last thing they would want is for someone to come snooping around."

"So you're saying that everything looks above board except

for the fact that they kill stolen cattle?"

"Yes. And the fact that they are most probably making a hell of a lot more than they're saying."

Nash suddenly had a thought. "Did you say the last name was Willis?"

"Yes, why?"

"When I had that issue with the two brothers on the way here there was another bloke with them. They called him Shit Head. His actual name was Stewart Henry Willis."

"Coincidence," Gloria said. "Byron Willis has three sons. Stewart, Brian, and Paul. All of them used to shoot kangaroos before the meat works was converted. Stewart still does."

"Add into the mix Olsen and it's a family affair. You don't think Moffat could be linked to them somehow?"

"I can check," Gloria told him.

"Thanks, babe."

"Anything else?"

"No."

"Then goodnight. Love you."

"Love you, too."

Nash came awake, his eyes suddenly open and staring at the ceiling faintly illuminated by the streetlights outside the pub. He lay there immobile. There was a reason this had happened but what it was, he had yet to determine.

He used all his will power to remain unmoving, giving the impression he was still asleep. His eyes darted around the room trying to see what had awakened him. At first it was a sound. The friction of fabric rubbing together. Then he saw the shadow on the wall creeping closer to the bed. He saw the arm straighten and the object in the figure's hand, an extension to the arm.

It was a handgun.

Nash rolled violently to the side away from the intruder just as the suppressed weapon coughed twice.

The PI hit the floor on the opposite side of the bed as more bullets punched into the wall behind him. He grabbed one of the pillows off the floor where he'd dumped it before going to bed and threw it at the figure.

As it sailed through the air, Nash followed it, scrambling across the bed as the shooter moved to dodge the object coming towards him.

Nash hit the would-be killer with his shoulder, feeling the impact jar through his body. The intruder reeled back, arms windmilling as he tried to keep his balance.

The former undercover grabbed for the killer's gun arm to prevent him from bringing it around to shoot at him again. The man was wearing gloves.

Nash forced him back, but the killer braced himself and slowed his movement. The handgun fired again, and a bullet punched through the ceiling, creating a small shower of plaster dust that rained upon the two struggling men.

Savagely, Nash brought his head forward, his forehead striking his attacker a solid blow. The killer grunted in pain and staggered momentarily. It was right then that Nash knew he was in trouble. This person was strong and had just taken one of his best blows. And he was still standing.

Suddenly blinding pain shot through Nash's body, radiating outward from his groin. Nausea swept over him, and he felt as though vomit would come hurtling up from his stomach at any moment.

His knees buckled and he started to slump to the carpeted floor. The killer broke his non-gun hand free of Nash's grasp and swung it at the PI's face. Knuckles grazed Nash's chin, inflicting little damage other than a contusion.

However, the killer's other hand broke free of his grip and Nash knew he only had moments to react before the man put a bullet in his head.

With a roar, he came to his feet, with all the power that remained in his legs thrusting him forward like pistons driving a locomotive. He hit the killer hard in the chest, driving him backward into a dresser with a mirror attached to it.

The mirror shattered under the impact as the dresser crunched into the wall. This time the killer let out a cry of pain as the edge of it caught him across the lower back.

Nash swung his right fist twice, his arm jarring severely under each impact. The killer grunted at both blows.

Something hard hit Nash in the side of his head and his ears started to ring. His eyes watered as he realized that it had to have been the gun.

A voice growled harshly, "Why don't you just die like your brother?"

That was all Nash needed to give him the power and determination to go on, his blood surging through his veins providing him almost superhuman strength.

Nash's vision cleared as the injection of adrenaline to his system charged around his body. He brought his fist through and lashed out, the knuckles crunching against his assailant's jaw.

For the next few moments, the battle ebbed and flowed and somehow, they got turned around. Nash, using all his remaining strength drove forward, the killer in a bearhug, his legs propelling him forward.

There was a shattering crash and the world seemed to turn upside down. Glass fell to the floor of the first-floor veranda, followed by the two men.

They hit the wood boards hard, Nash feeling a sharp sting in his right arm as a shard of glass pierced the flesh. Beneath him the killer cried out in pain, obviously sustaining more substantial injuries than the private investigator.

Nash dragged himself to his feet slowly. He staggered about trying to regain his balance as the world tilted drunkenly first one way and then the other. In front of him, the killer did the same. In the orange streetlight, Nash caught a glimpse of the man's face. Blood, pouring from a gash on his forehead, ran down his face, then trickled across his lips, giving his ugly sneer a truly macabre look.

In his right hand, the killer retained the gun he'd used to wound the ceiling, trying to kill the private investigator. Without thinking, Nash charged him again, his shoulder connecting with the man's guts. Once more, both men were propelled towards a precipice.

With a loud crack the balustrade on the veranda gave way and both men toppled into oblivion.

Nash felt someone slapping his face and his eyes snapped open. Above him was a pretty face that he recognized straight away. It was Constable Eleanor Parker. "Well, at least you're still alive. That's one thing."

Nash moaned. "Where did he go?"

"Where did who go?"

"The bloke who was in my room. The killer."

That got her attention. "What killer? What are you talking about?"

"The hitman, the one that killed my brother? And most likely a string of others from between here and Adelaide."

"Shit." She stood up and walked away. Nash could hear her speaking into her radio but couldn't make out what she was saying.

"That's some fall you took there, Dave Nash."

Nash's blood ran cold as he recognized the voice. He turned his head to see Smith standing over him. "I wouldn't recommend it."

"The constable tells me you're a private investigator. Care to fucking elaborate?"

"Maybe not right now, but we'll have that talk."

An ambulance pulled into a parking spot outside the pub, its blue and red lights flashing. Two paramedics climbed out and knelt beside Nash and began asking him questions as they examined his body.

"Looks like you have a few nasty cuts there, chief," one of them said. She was a middle-aged woman who looked like she'd been out in the sun too long. "Can you tell me where it hurts?"

"I'll be fine," Nash said and tried to sit up.

A gloved hand, planted in the middle of his chest, held him in place. "Not so fast like, we need to get you sorted out. You'll have to come into the medical center. From there, you'll be assessed as to whether you need to be transported to Meekatharra for proper treatment."

"I tell you I'm fine."

There was a rattle and a crash as the second Ambo retrieved a gurney from the back of the vehicle. A few minutes later, they had him strapped on, then into the back of the ambulance. Before they closed the doors, Nash said, "Smith, come down to the medical center."

Then the doors closed, and Nash was gone.

A couple of hours and a few stitches later, Nash put his shirt on and was doing up the buttons when Constable Parker entered the cubicle. Smith was sitting off to one side in a chair. She glanced at him and then back at Nash. "Detectives are going to want to talk to you, so don't leave town."

"I have a job I have to get back to," Nash said, giving Smith a quick glance. "I gave you a description."

She gave him a stare before saying, "I want you at the station in three hours. That's nine o'clock. Understood?"

Nash nodded. "Fine. I'll be there."

She turned and left. Then after a minute of silence, Smith asked, "You want to tell me what the fuck is going on?"

"Depends," the private investigator said.

"Depends on what?"

"On whether I can trust you to keep your mouth shut. But I suppose you can, because I know your secret. Just like you know mine."

Smith glared at him, unimpressed with the veiled threat. "I don't know shit about you, mate."

"That's right, you don't."

"Fuck."

Nash thought for a moment before saying, "What I'm about to tell you goes no further than you and me. If it does, it'll bring me a world of pain. I'll then take that pain and use it against you. Do you understand?"

"Yes, OK." There was frustration in the young station hand's voice.

"As you already know, my name is Dave Nash. I'm a private investigator. I used to be an undercover copper for the federal police."

"Shit a brick."

"Just shut up. I'm not finished," Nash reprimanded him. "A short time back, my niece and her boyfriend went missing. Apparently, they were last seen out at Moffat Station. Her name was Tiffany. His was Rory. Couple of days ago they found her body. She'd been shot with a high-powered rifle and dumped. Then yesterday, I found his body while I was out checking a water hole. He'd been dead for a while. I told Moffat, and I told Olsen. They said they were going to get the police to have a look at it, but I highly doubt they did. Given what's going on out there."

While Nash had been speaking, Smith's face had grown paler and paler. The private investigator said, "I know you know what I'm talking about."

Smith gave a slight shake of his head. "Spell it out."

"Really? Cattle rustling, stealing, whatever you want to call it. They're using the place to fatten up the cattle before they move them on. And don't tell me it's not true, because I know. I took pictures of brands and traced them back."

Smith looked guilty. "All right. So you know what's going on."

"Listen, I don't give a fuck about the cattle. What I care about is what happened to my niece. Start talking."

"I remember them," Smith said. "They got nosey and found out what was going on."

"What happened?"

"Fine, I'll tell you."

MOFFAT STATION
BEFORE...

Tiffany urgently stuffed clothes into her backpack as Rory came in through the door. His face was a mask of panic. "What are you doing? Forget about that. We've got to go now."

"But what about our stuff?"

"Forget it. Just come on."

"I knew this was a bad idea," Tiffany cried.

"How were we to know they had a stolen cattle ring going on out here?"

Rory grabbed her by the hand and pulled her outside onto the veranda. It was dark and he could hear voices shouting from over near the cattle pens. "Come on, let's go."

"Where, Rory? Where are we going to go?"

"We'll head towards the road to see if we can pick up a ride."

"Going somewhere?" Olsen emerged from the darkness cradling a high-powered rifle. The young station hand Terry Smith was beside him.

"We are leaving," said Rory. "You can't stop us."

Olsen raised his eyebrows. "Really? I always knew you two were going to be trouble. Just too nosey for your own good. I should have just turned you away when you arrived. I guess it's too late now."

"What are you talking about?" Smith asked.

"Well, shit, Terry. Do you think we can just let them go after they've seen what they have, and know what they do?"

"They didn't say anything," Smith told him.

"Can't take that chance, can we?"

"What are you going to do?"

"What the fuck do you think? Have you got shit for brains

or something?"

"You can't just kill them."

"If you don't have the stomach for it, fuck off."

"But they don't know anything," Smith insisted.

"Do you really think that? He was over at the cattle yards. He heard us all talking."

"But they don't know what we do with them. Hell, I don't even know what we do with them."

"And that is the way it is going to stay."

"Please don't kill us," Tiffany begged. "We won't say anything. We don't know anything. You must believe us."

However, there was to be no reasoning with the foreman and Rory could sense it. In an act of desperation, he leaped forward and crashed into Olsen, knocking him from his feet.

"Run, Tiffy!" he shouted.

Tiffany ran as fast as she could into the darkness. Rory followed close behind her. Olsen scrambled to his feet and began firing his rifle after them. But they were gone.

PRESENT DAY...

"Well, one of those bullets must have found him," Nash growled.

"I tried to stop him. Honest."

"Not hard enough."

Smith mumbled something unintelligible.

"My niece was found out at the Bluffs. Know where that is?"

Smith nodded. "Long way from here."

"Yeah, well."

"No, you don't understand, Nash. The Bluffs are a long way from the station, too. She wouldn't have made it that far on foot."

Nash suddenly understood what he was saying. "She was taken there?"

"Had to have been," Smith replied.

"Olsen?"

"I don't know."

"Can you take me out there?"

"We have to get back," Smith pointed out.

"We will, eventually," Nash assured him.

"Shit. Don't you have a detective to see?"

"Yeah, one day."

CHAPTER FOURTEEN

THE BLUFFS

The landscape was a deep red, covered with eucalypts and dry spinifex. The Bluffs were exactly what Harris had told him they were. Two small plateaus standing out against the panoramic vista.

Smith brought the Land Cruiser to a stop at the base of the first bluff. Both men climbed out of the vehicle and stood staring at their surroundings. "What now?" Smith asked.

"We look around."

The police were obviously finished with their investigations because there was no sign of them or anything else. Nash started to walk away from the Land Cruiser, taking a circuitous route around the two bluffs. Smith walked with him, the pair of them scanning the ground as they went, looking for any evidence of what might have befallen Tiffany.

"What exactly are we looking for?"

"I'll know it when I find it."

"Are you going to turn me in to the police?" Smith asked.

"I haven't decided yet." Which was true. Part of Nash wanted to; he knew he should. But there was another part of him that felt sorry for the young man who'd been caught up in everything that was going on. And like he said, he'd tried to stop it. But obviously not hard enough.

"You never said who the guy was at the hotel."

"He's a hitman hired to kill me."

"What the fuck? What the hell did you do?"

"A while back I got into a little bit of trouble. There was this crime figure, a woman. She had two sons who thought they were better than what they were. Things happened and I killed them. Now she's after revenge. She's already killed my brother and his wife. Plus, numerous others."

"And this guy has followed you all this way to here."

"That's about it." Nash suddenly became aware of the aches and pains and of the stitches pulling as he walked along.

"Well, maybe he'll leave you alone now after last night."

Nash shook his head. "Not likely. It's not how they work. He'll keep coming until either the job's done or he can't come any more. It's gonna end up one of two ways: with me dead or him. That's just the way it is."

The private investigator hadn't told him about Gloria, deciding that he didn't need to know. That way it gave him an ace up his sleeve, just in case he needed her. That was the other thing. He hadn't called her either to tell her about his run-in the night before with the intruder.

Nash stopped, lifted his gaze and ran his eyes around his surroundings. The landscape was undulating, not flat like one would expect it to be. "Is there any other way into this place other than the one that we've just come in on?"

"There are three ways. One to the north. And another to the Northeast, not that anyone uses it. It's just an overgrown track."

"Show me."

They walked for about a kilometer before coming across it. It was barely visible through the spinifex and the rocks, but it was there. Nash stood for a moment, looking at it. Then back over his shoulder at the Bluffs. He started walking away from the craggy-faced escarpments following the ghost track. "This way."

They followed the track for another hundred or so meters before Nash stopped. He pointed at the ground. "There, see it?"

Smith stared at the track for a moment before nodding. "Barely."

It was only faint, but it was perceptible. A single tire mark on a sandy patch no bigger than a dinner plate. "Someone was here."

For the next twenty minutes, as though he was performing a grid search like he had done as a constable in the New South Wales Police Force, Nash searched for more sign. He was about to give up when he saw it. Just a fine glint of sunlight off something shiny. He walked over to it and bent down.

As Smith watched him, Nash broke off a small twig before

using it to lift the object up to eye height. It was a spent bullet casing.

"Winchester three-oh-eight," Nash said, turning around, looking back towards the Bluffs. "I'm guessing the crime scene is down there somewhere. Whoever it was, shot her from up here."

"Why didn't the police find it?" Smith asked.

"Who knows? Maybe they didn't search this far out. Maybe they were just lazy."

"What are you going to do with it?"

"Find something to put it in and then take it into the police station."

"So you're still going there?" Smith asked.

"I am now."

Suddenly, something cracked close to their heads. Nash knew immediately what it was, then shoved Smith to the ground. "Get down!"

Almost immediately, the sound reached out again. This time, moments afterwards he heard the report from the rifle.

"Shit!" Smith exclaimed. "Are we being shot at?"

"Yes, don't move."

Nash slowly looked around. Further, along the track, he could see a low ridge, some 800 meters in the distance. As he looked at it, he saw a small flash. Had to be sunlight off a riflescope. "Whoever it is, is up there on the ridge. Just keep still."

Another shot came in. This time the bullet buried itself about five meters to Nash's right, kicking up a small puff of red dust. Again, the report from the rifle followed soon after. Nash turned his head and looked behind him. He spied a shallow gully there where water runoff had scoured away the topsoil over many years. It wasn't much, but it would give them cover.

"Smith, you see that gully back there?"

"Yes."

"We need to get to it."

"How do you propose we do that with this asshole shooting at us?" he asked.

"Just run like hell and don't look back. And don't run in a straight line."

"If you say so."

"Are you ready?" Nash asked him.

"No."

"Go!"

Both men came to their feet and started to run, zigzagging as they went.

Another rifle shot rang out. Nash felt the passage of the bullet as it whizzed past his head. The distance they had to cover was only about twenty meters, but it felt like two hundred with each stride. It was like that dream when you're trying to run away from a snake, and the faster you try to run, the slower you go until eventually the reptile bites you.

With each step Nash's expectation of feeling a bullet slam him between the shoulder blades rose, and had he thought about it, would have been pleasantly surprised that with his last desperate dive, launching himself into the gully, that he was bullet free. He did, however, feel his stitches give and the bite of sharp stones in his hands and legs, even through the thick denim of his jeans. He bit back a curse as pain tore through his body, remnants of his set-to from the night before.

Nash realized Smith was beside him and said, "Are you alright?"

"I'm not dead, so I guess that's a good thing," he replied. "Do you think it's your mate from last night?"

"I doubt it. There's no way he could get out here around through back here, back that way. My guess is that someone doesn't want us snooping around here."

Then Nash realized that the shooting had stopped. He crept along a few paces before slowly raising his head above the edge of the gully to peer over. He looked and saw nothing. "I think whoever it was is gone. We'll give it a little more time and then we'll head off."

"What happened to the bullet casing you found?"

Nash cursed with the sudden realization that he had been holding it in his hand, his palm wrapped tightly around it. He put it in his pocket, but the damage was already done. All he could do was hope that forensics could find something.

They lay there for the next 20 minutes before, finally, Nash shrugged and stood up. He tensed as he did so, half expecting a bullet to come flying out of the vast expanse before him and punch into his chest.

He let out a slow breath, relief flooding him. "You can stand up, Terry."

Smith came to his feet. "Let's get out of here."

Nash shook his head. "Not yet."

"What do you mean, not yet? We had some bastard just shooting at us and you want to hang around. Like fuck, I'm gone."

Nash nodded. "That's fine. Go back to the Land Cruiser. I'll be along soon. I just want to check it out."

"You're crazy, you know that?"

"Been told that more times than I care to count," Nash said as he started towards the ridge.

"I thought you were going back to the Land Cruiser?" Nash called over his shoulder as he walked along.

In a eucalypt somewhere off to his right a crow laughed at him as though he sensed the pair were walking to their deaths. Something startled it, and it took flight, heading away from the pair towards the east.

Nash stopped. He heard a growl coming from behind the spinifex where the crow had taken flight. "Hold it, Terry."

The station hand stopped beside Nash. They waited for what seemed like an age before they saw the dog. It was a big brute of a thing. Sandy and white with large, brown-colored eyes.

But what drew Nash's attention was the leather chest plate it wore which would serve as protection against wild animals such as feral pigs. "Somebody's hunting dog," Nash said. "Have you seen it before?"

"I'm not sure."

"You're not sure? Or you have?"

"I might have."

The animal gave another low growl from deep within its chest. Nash looked around for a large rock, something that he might use to defend himself against it. "How fast can you run?"

"With that thing after me, I'll grow wings."

"That's no good. I was hoping you'd be slower than me."

"Fine time for a joke."

Nash raised his eyebrows. "Who was being funny?"

But instead of attacking them, the beast turned and loped away. Nash gave a sigh of relief. "Fuck it, let's get out of here. I've seen enough."

"I'm with you."

When they reached the Land Cruiser, Nash said, "You didn't tell me whose dog it was."

"That's because I wasn't sure."

"Well, are you now?"

"No."

"Tell me anyway."

"I think the dog belongs to Bullshit Willis."

Things were starting to come together.

"Let me run something past you. Byron Willis is the owner of a meat works northwest of Meekatharra. Olsen is his nephew. Olsen comes to work at Moffat Station about the same time that Byron Willis's meat works starts processing cattle and some pet food."

"I wouldn't know that. I haven't been there that long, remember?"

"Fair enough. Let me ask you this. Could the cattle be going to the meat works?"

"I suppose."

"What do you know about Cowral Cattle?"

"The livestock haulers?"

"Yes."

"Nothing except for the ones that bring the cattle in and the cattle out."

Nash nodded. "Where do they operate from?"

"Meekatharra." Smith frowned. "What has stolen cattle got to do with your niece's death?"

"I'm not sure, but somehow, I get the feeling that the two are connected. Come on, let's head back to town."

As soon as he had reception, Nash rang Gloria. When she answered, she said, "I was starting to think you'd forgotten about me."

"I could never forget about you."

"Where are you? You sound like you're driving."

"I'm not, someone else is."

"What's going on?" There was concern in her voice now.

"Long story, I'll tell you later. However, I do need the wonderful mother of my child to do something for me."

"You're a suck. What is it?"

"Look into Cowral Cattle Cartage. They operate out of Meekatharra."

"Are they the ones shipping the cattle?"

"Yes. I need you to see if you can find out where they take them. I'm guessing it is the meat works."

"I'll go out there and have a look around."

"That' not wise, Gloria."

"What could possibly go wrong, Nash?"

"Christ. Be aware that Willis's sons are in this up to their eyeballs somehow. I think one of them is our killer."

"It's a good thing I have my Glock then, isn't it?"

"I'm serious, Gloria. These people are not to be fucked around with."

"Neither am I. I'll tell you when I've got some news."

"Be careful, babe."

By the time the call disconnected, they were on the edge of town. Smith drove straight to the police station, where they both climbed out and went inside. Constable Eleanor Parker looked up from some paperwork she was doing and stared at both of them. However, her hardest stare was reserved for Nash. "Where the hell have you been?"

"Getting shot at. How about you?"

"I'm not in the mood for your smartarse comments, Nash. Now tell me where have you been? The detectives were here and when you weren't, they climbed so far up my ass I could taste their breath."

"I said we were getting shot at."

She frowned. "Where?"

"Out at the Bluffs."

Parker picked up a notepad off a desk and then stood up,

coming across to the counter where both men stood. She raised a small trap door and stepped aside, saying, "You'd better come in and take a seat."

They followed her instructions and sat down in the vacant chairs opposite her. While they did this, she stuck her head into the sergeant's office and then made a call to the detectives. Nash looked at Smith and said, "I guess we're not going back to work today."

Halliday emerged from his office and stared at both men. "What are you doing here, Terry?" he asked.

"I don't rightly know."

"Alright. What's this about you getting shot at? And why the fuck weren't you here when you were supposed to be?" The tone of the last part harsher as he stared at Nash.

Nash filled him in.

"What were you doing out there?"

"Trying to find out what happened to my niece."

"You were told to leave it to the detectives."

Nash's face grew hard. "The detectives haven't done shit. If they had, they would have found what I did."

"And what is it you found?"

He reached into his pocket and took out the bullet casing. "It's a three-oh-eight Winchester."

"Where did you find it?"

Nash told him.

"You realize any trace evidence that was on that is probably useless about now?"

"No shit, Sherlock. Wasn't really thinking about that when

some prick was trying to shoot me. I was hoping maybe some forensics might be able to be gotten off it. If they find anything."

"I'll see what I can do. Did you see who was shooting at you?"

"No."

Just then two familiar faces appeared. Detectives Power and Harvey. The latter stared at Nash and said, "You're just a shit storm constantly regenerating, aren't you?"

"Are you saying I caused all this?" Nash asked incredulously.

"Wouldn't have happened if you weren't here."

"Fuck you, asshole."

Harvey took a step closer, and the move forced Halliday to step in between them. "Keep it civil, gentlemen. Parker, take Mister Nash through to the interview room. Smith, in my office."

Parker escorted Nash through to the interview room and sat him down at the table in there. "Would you like a drink?"

"Coffee?"

"I'll get you one. Sugar?"

"One."

"Milk?"

"Please."

"Back shortly."

She left the room, but Nash wasn't on his own for long. Harvey and Power entered followed by Halliday. "Remember, this is my station. Play nice or I'll kick the lot of you out."

Harvey glared at him but said nothing.

"I don't care if you do outrank me." He closed the door behind him, and the two officers took up their positions. Nash figured they'd probably rehearsed it many times. Harvey sat across from him while Power took up a pose in the corner of the room behind Nash's right shoulder.

The former undercover turned his head and said, "Move or I walk."

"What?"

"I'm here because I want to be. Try intimidating me and I'll say fuck you and leave."

"You leave when we say so," Harvey said. "By the way, I saw your other half in Meekatharra. She was busy interfering in our investigation. Trying to compromise it."

"That's where you're wrong," Nash said casually. "She's doing your job for you because you're fucking useless."

Nash had had enough. Everything that had been brewing within him was starting to come out and there was a big fat target in front of him.

"Stay away from it. I won't tell you again."

The door to the interview room opened and another detective walked in. This one wore a black suit and had hair to match. He was tall, and solidly built. He nodded at Harvey.

Harvey said, "David Nash this is Detective Inspector Len Miller. He's in charge of Major Crimes. At the moment he's overseeing several investigations of which you seem to be at the center. The most important being the hitman who is leaving a trail of bodies behind him hundreds of kilometers long."

"Mister Nash."

"Inspector."

"Tell us what happened last night."

"I had a fight. Bloke tried to kill me, and I threw him out a window."

"Threw yourself out of it, too, I'm told."

Suddenly Nash became aware of a nagging pain in his head, possibly leftover remnants of a concussion. "Not by choice."

Miller nodded. "I've done some looking into you, Nash."

"Wouldn't be doing your job if you didn't."

"You've done some good things over the course of your career. Some stupid ones as well."

"When you do what I did, sometimes you don't get much of a choice."

"You mean undercover?"

"Yes. You ever do it?"

"No. Not on the scale you did."

"It leaves its mark."

"I'm sure it does. Now, tell me about last night."

Nash filled him in, telling him all that he knew. When he was done, Miller nodded slowly. "What I'm about to tell you remains in this room. It can't get out, is that understood?"

"Do you think it's wise, sir?" Harvey asked.

"It my decision to make, Lee," Miller said curtly.

"Yes, sir."

"I'll ask you again, Mister Nash. Do you understand?"

Nash nodded and straightened in his chair. "Yes."

"Fine. It seems that our killer got a little sloppy at one of the crime scenes. Trace evidence found has led us to a suspect who we believe may be responsible for at least six other murders on top of these latest ones he's wanted for. Later this evening we are going to release a picture and name to go with it."

"Who is he?"

"Man named Joe Black. Former soldier."

Nash remained silent.

"We will also be posting a reward for information which we hope will bring about a swift result."

"Hopefully," Nash said.

"Lee and Roger were telling me that you were here looking for your niece. I'm sorry for your loss."

Nash nodded.

"They also said you have a theory."

"It's a refined theory."

"You've got a captive audience, Mister Nash. I'm listening."

"The latter killings were all done by the same person or persons."

"How do you figure that?" Miller asked. "It's all been looked at."

"Looked at poorly," Nash replied. "Bordering on incompetence."

"That's a big accusation, Nash," Harvey blurted.

"You should know, I gave you the folder."

Miller cleared his throat. "I don't care what's in the folder. I'm asking you."

"All right. At first, I was looking at the bigger picture right back to around twenty-ten. After all, we all know that killers can adapt, and maybe they have. I know that's what Maria

Gallagher believed."

"The reporter?"

"Yes. Her story made me think that there was something to it and that Tiffany and Rory might have fallen victim to a serial killer."

"And now?"

"I'm not sure," Nash lied.

"What about the others?" Miller asked.

"My partner, Gloria—"

"Senior Constable Gloria Browning?"

"Yes. She gave me the idea that I should concentrate on the more recent ones because they had a lot more in common to link them. Things that the investigating officers should have picked up on."

"Such as?"

"Have you seen the folder?"

"Again, I'm asking you."

"Back as far as twenty-fifteen the victims had dog bites," Nash told him. "There was also the case of the Aboriginal girl who was hit by a truck further north. The driver says there was a possibility she was being chased by a dog. You might want to send Laurel and Hardy back to Meekatharra to ask him some more questions."

"It's wild country out there," Miller pointed out. "Plenty of dingoes and wild dogs."

"They were all around the legs. I think if you check with the medical examiner in Meekatharra now he might have a different opinion since talking to Gloria."

Miller glanced at Harvey. The detective nodded. "He seems to think that there is a good possibility that they are linked."

"Shit," Miller muttered.

"They were hunted, Inspector15," Nash said. "They were all killed in different ways, but they were hunted none the less."

"That's your theory."

"Call it whatever you want, it still doesn't change the fact."

"Do you have any idea who might be responsible?" Miller asked.

"No," he lied.

"All right," said Miller. "I'd like you to hang around town for a few days if that's all right with you?"

"I was kind of in the middle of something," Nash said casually.

Miller looked at him quizzically. "What kind of something?"

"Who do you know in Rural Crimes?"

CHAPTER FIFTEEN

MOUNT WARRIGAL
WESTERN AUSTRALIA

"Absolutely not," Harvey growled. "He's got nothing to do with West Australian police."

"Think of me as an informant," Nash said. "Besides, it's not as if I haven't done it before."

"He's right, Lee," Miller said. "He's already in place."

"But what does he want in return?" Power asked suspiciously.

Nash smiled. "I'm glad you asked. First, the young station hand in Halliday's office. He works out there and got mixed up in something he knew nothing about at the time. He also is wanted in Queensland on a trumped-up charge which needs sorting out."

Miller said, "I can't promise anything, but I'll see what I can do. Is there anything else?"

"An officer for Gloria. If that prick found me, then he could find her."

"Where is she?"

"Meekatharra. I'll let you know the address after I call her."

"Anything else." This time the tone of voice indicated that to ask for anything more would be pushing his luck.

"I don't think so. I'll bring you up to speed and we can go from there."

"You need to wear a wire," Harvey said.

"Fuck off. I can't do my job and wear a wire."

"I agree," said Miller. "No wire. But I do expect regular updates."

"I can do that."

Miller nodded. "Fine, then we have a deal."

"I want a gun." Nash's voice was adamant.

Harvey stared at Miller urging him not to.

Miller said, "I'm sure we can find you a rifle."

Nash shook his head. "No, get me a Glock with spare clips and ammunition."

"Listen, Nash, I don't—"

"These people are dangerous. I'm sure they've killed and possibly will again."

The inspector looked suspicious. "What aren't you telling us?"

"Nothing yet," Nash lied.

"Nash, if you're holding something back, I'll can this right now."

"I found Rory Williams's body."

"What the fuck?" Harvey exploded.

"You'd better fill me in, Mister Nash," Miller said.

Nash told them all he knew about the body and what had happened that night. When he was done, Harvey said, "I'll get a team organized."

"No," Nash snapped. "The body isn't going anywhere, and we have a witness who will swear to what happened. There's still more to this investigation. If you go stomping around out there now, we may never know who killed Tiffany."

"What do you mean?" Miller asked. "She was obviously killed by this Olsen bloke."

"Maybe, but there is a chance that she wasn't. She was shot with a three-oh-eight. Let me see if I can find one on the station. If there is one, then we know for sure."

"Would Smith know what Olsen uses?" Miller asked.

"Maybe. I never asked."

The inspector looked across at Power. "Go and get him."

The detective left the interview room and Miller focused once more on Nash. "You should have told us about the body, Nash."

"Maybe, but I didn't want you lot to go charging in there and muddying the waters."

"This is one big fucking mess. Is there anything else you're holding back?"

"No." Another lie.

A few moments later, Smith was shown into the room. He looked nervously at the men and then at Nash. "What is this about?"

"What rifle does Olsen use, Terry?" Nash asked.

"A two-four-three."

"Not a three-oh-eight?"

"No," he replied with a shake of his head.

Nash nodded. "There you go."

Miller shook his head. "So we've got a hitman on the loose, a stock stealing operation which is responsible for the death of at least one person that we know of, and now it looks like a serial killer."

"That's about the size of it."

"Tell me this, Nash. What happened to your niece between the time she left the station, and when she was murdered?"

"I wish I knew."

BEFORE...

Tiffany ran like there wasn't any tomorrow. Through the darkness she stumbled and fell over unseen objects. It was at least an hour since she had been separated from Rory. He'd told her to keep going, that he would catch up, but he never did; now she was out here frightened, alone, and exhausted. The adrenalin from her flight had finally left her system, extreme fatigue the outcome.

At one point she had seen the headlights of a vehicle bouncing over the rugged terrain. But then they disappeared, moving off, to her relief, in another direction. She was thirsty, tired, and had no idea where she was at all. Just that if she kept going the way she was, she would find the road and eventual help.

In the east a thin orange line started to appear just above the horizon. Tiffany stopped and stared at it. It was on her right. She stomped her foot in frustration; she'd been going the wrong way. Traveling north because somehow the darkness had turned her around and she'd lost her sense of direction.

But she also had another problem. Now that the sun was coming up, she either needed water or a place to stop until it got dark again. If she continued her trek through the heat of the day, it would kill her.

But where?

By the time the sun was fully risen she still hadn't found a place to hide. Now the flies were swarming all around her, chasing any moisture her body emitted with the rising temperature of the day.

Tiffany wasn't sure how she was still moving, stumbling on weary legs without the strength to lift her feet properly, her boots kicking loose rocks aside rather than stepping over them, stirring small puffs of red dust with her passage.

Just ahead, beckoning her like an oasis was a small stand of eucalypts in the middle of the copper-colored landscape, offering her some kind of shade.

She heard it before she saw it, then the dust seemed to billow from the ground in its wake. A vehicle, most likely a 4X4. Tiffany dropped to her knee and waited to see which way it would go.

As it grew closer, she narrowed her eyes against the glare

of the sun. It was indeed a 4X4. A white one. But it wasn't one from the station. Her heart raced. She came to her feet and started running, stumbling, waving her arms. "Help! Over here! Help me!"

For a moment it looked as though the vehicle was going to drive on by, but it soon changed direction and came towards her. Relief washed over Tiffany. She was safe. Whoever it was would take her to the police and then they could find Rory.

Overcome with exhaustion, she sat down and cried.

THE PRESENT...

"Where are you?" Nash asked Gloria.

"I'm at the motel. I'm not going to the meat works until tomorrow. Why?"

"Forget it. There will be a police officer coming for you in the morning to bring you back to Mount Warrigal."

"What's going on, Nash?" There was concern in her voice, even if she was using his last name again.

He related some details, conveniently omitting certain things because of ears within earshot. "We'll talk more the next time we see each other."

"What do you want me to do about the things I'm supposed to be looking into?" Gloria asked.

"Which ones?"

There was a pause. "Is somebody listening?"

"Uh, huh."

"The meat works?"

"No."

"The cattle cartage company?"

"Can you?"

"I think so."

"OK."

"You just be careful," she said to him.

"You know me."

"Yes, I do."

The call disconnected and Nash looked over at Miller.

"It's all fine. She'll be expecting your officer in the morning."

The superintendent nodded. "Right, let's get you and your friend back to the station."

"Where the fuck have you been?" Olsen growled, his eyes narrowing as he stared at the two men before him. It was dark by an hour when they returned. "Give me one good reason why I shouldn't fire you here and now. Especially you, Nash?"

"We had car problems," Smith lied. The police had set up a backstop which would hold before they were let go.

"You never heard of a fucking phone? Or were you both too drunk?"

"Look, if you don't believe us," Nash said, "call the mechanic and find out."

"Maybe I will."

"Go right ahead."

"Shit," Olsen hissed. "Get inside, Nash. Smith, over to the yards, we've got a truck coming in."

"Tonight?"

"Yes. It'll be here in an hour. Get moving."

"I'll just get rid of this other gear."

"Hurry up."

Nash and Smith went to their bunk room. Nash asked, "You look confused."

"That's because I am. Trucks never come in on short notice. Usually, we get plenty of time. Besides, one went out of here last night."

"You sure?"

"Yes."

"I might have a look around," Nash said.

Smith's eyes widened. "That's not a good idea."

"It's the only way to learn things," Nash replied. "I'll be careful."

"Shit."

Smith headed off to prepare for the unexpected arrival. Nash remained inside his room and waited for the truck to come. When the growl of the big engine was audible, he turned out the lights and slipped outside.

Nash used the sheds and outbuildings for cover as he circled around to the yards. By the time he got there the truck had backed in its first trailer and the hands were starting to unload the bottom deck.

Nash watched on as the trailer emptied out under a floodlight. They pushed them into a back pen and readied to unload the top deck.

He heard Smith ask one of the other hands, "What's with the load?"

"Too many coppers on the highway, had to bring it back."

Nash knew what he meant.

"What now?" another asked.

"We put them out into one of the back paddocks until things quiet down. Nothing else coming in or out."

"I bet the boss isn't happy."

"Not much he can do about it. Been a spate of killings and like I said, coppers everywhere."

As the top deck started to unload, Nash moved around the yards so he could see the cattle in the back pen. They were Black Angus and very healthy-looking animals. He checked the brands under the weak light spreading across the back pen.

A voice called out from nearby and he dropped low as he tried to keep out of sight. He memorized the brand he saw and would put it down on paper later.

Nash moved back into the shadows and paused. A hand appeared and Nash froze. The man looked around then called over his shoulder, "We'll need to use the other pens, we're out of room in this one."

The former undercover waited for a few more minutes for the hand to go. Then he was about to move when he sensed someone close. He tensed and whirled, about to explode in violence when he saw the dim light on the face of Werner.

"What the fuck are you doing?" Nash hissed.

"What are you doing?" he shot back in a low voice.

"Shit, follow me."

They started walking away when Werner knocked over a stack of empty twenty-liter drums. The noise sounded deafening, and Nash stopped dead. He waited for someone to call out but all he heard was the lowing of the cattle.

He grabbed Werner by the shoulder and began dragging him along. "Come on, before we're both fucked," he hissed.

When they reached relative safety behind one of the sheds, they stopped, and Nash spun to face the German. Nash was livid; if anyone could stuff things up, it was Werner. "You need to stay away from me."

"Why?"

"Because I fucking said so."

"But Emma is missing."

Nash stopped. "What do you mean?"

"I cannot find her," Werner explained.

"How long?"

"Since yesterday. What should I do?"

"Did you ask that bloke she was seeing?"

Werner went silent as he dropped his head, his wounds still raw. Then, "No."

"Don't you think you should ask him?"

"I will go now."

Nash grabbed his arm. "Shit, not now. Christ."

"What are they doing, anyway?" Werner asked.

"Something you'd best be staying clear of. Come on, let's get back to the bunkhouse."

Nash led the way, using the buildings and dark shadows to

return, except when they did, someone was already waiting for them.

"Well, well, well," Olsen said.

"Three holes in the ground," Nash shot back at him aware of the rifle the foreman held in his hand.

"Where the fuck have you two bastards been?"

"Out the back for a piss?" Nash said. "Saving water."

"Bullshit. I think you've been sticking your nose in where it ain't wanted. Huh?"

Werner stepped forward. "Nein, we were—"

The rifle moved, slamming into the German's middle. He grunted, doubled over, and sank to the dirt, moaning in pain.

Nash knelt beside the fallen man. "You rotten mongrel bas—"

Then Nash's words came to an abrupt halt as the rifle fell.

CHAPTER SIXTEEN

MEEKATHARRA
WESTERN AUSTRALIA

The latch clicked open, and the door sprang back just a touch. Gloria poked her head in and looked around the darkened room. As she stepped into the office, she knew that should she be caught, things could go badly two ways. She could be taken away and possibly killed. Or she could be handed over to the police and her career would be royally screwed.

Gloria closed the door and reached into her pocket for her flashlight. The tall floodlight from outside never really pierced the blinds on the inside so it was relatively dark. She pressed the button and it lit up the office. She shielded it with her hand so if a security vehicle from one of the local services decided to swing by on its rounds, it wouldn't be tipped off.

"Where do we start, Gloria?" she muttered to herself.

She walked over to a desk and opened the drawers. They

mostly contained stationery, nothing much else of importance. She moved a few things around and checked a diary which held only appointments.

Shining the flashlight around the room she saw an old steel filing cabinet against the wall. There was a good chance it would be locked but she shrugged and crossed to it. Gloria reached for the top pull and gave it a gentle tug.

The rusted glides made the drawer grate loudly in protest as it slid out jerkily, making her raise her eyebrows. "Well, what do you know?"

She spent the next few minutes flicking through each drawer but found nothing of any use.

Once more the light danced around and stopped on a closed door. The sign on it said: KEEP OUT!

"Nothing says welcome like that."

She walked over to the door and tried the knob. It was locked. Of course it was, all the interesting ones are.

Gloria turned, placing her back against the door. She leaned forward a touch, then bringing a right foot up, she drove it backwards with sufficient force to pop the lock. "And that, ladies and gents, is how you open doors."

On the other side of the door was a smaller, private office. The walls held large charts and a white board with numbers on it. It also had a desk and a filing cabinet which was newer than the one in the outer office.

She walked over to the desk and tried one of the drawers. It slid open easily and she looked inside. Nothing. Next came the filing cabinet, and Gloria was surprised to find it wasn't locked. She rifled through it, looking for anything which might point her in the right direction. What she found was a large Collins hardcover ledger. She took it out and opened it, running a finger down the columns at the numbers and names. "This is interesting."

Gloria tucked it under her arm and then closed the drawer. She shone the flashlight onto the large whiteboard and looked at all the names, numbers, letters and columns. She took out her cell and then took a photo of it, making sure that she got it all in. It might be nothing, but it could be something. She would look at it later.

After a few more minutes, Gloria was gone.

Back in her motel room, Gloria made a coffee and sat on the bed going through the ledger. At first everything looked above board. However, after a while, she started picking up small discrepancies. One customer seemed to have more cattle going in and none going out. A little further digging told her it was the meat works. Nothing out of place, except the transport prices. Someone had been careless.

One-hundred head of cattle from a property south of Perth had the same cartage charge as another from a station no more than a hundred kilometers away. Then a third from a property further north, same amount paid for seventy head.

Gloria checked the brand numbers and looked at the Western Australia Brand and PIC Register. They matched, which meant that everything looked all official and on the up. Except for the amount paid.

She checked her watch. It was 10pm. She shrugged and found a phone number for the first station. Ti-Tree Downs which operated under Southwest Pastoral Holdings and was owned by a Darrell Green.

"Yeah?" The voice sounded tired, grumpy.

"I'm sorry to ring you so late, sir," Gloria said apologetically. "My name is…is Francis McCafferty from—"

"Who?"

"Francis McCafferty."

"Look, girlie, make it quick. A man has to be up at five. Can't it bloody wait?"

"Sorry. Really sorry. A new girl at our office today spilled coffee all over our books at work here and I'm trying to get them fixed before the boss finds out and shitcans both of us. I—"

"Just get on with it. I don't care about the ins and outs."

"Yes, sorry. Did you recently sell a hundred head of cattle to—"

"No." His voice was firm, definite.

"Are you sure?"

"I own the bloody things, don't I?" Green snapped. "We've been in drought for nearly two years. I need good rain before I even dream about selling one damn scarecrow."

Gloria nodded. "Thank you, sir, sorry to bother you."

The call disconnected with a grunt from Green.

Gloria knew she possibly had what she needed but knew one more call would confirm it all.

She made it and got the same answer. There had been no sale of cattle in the past six months. For the next hour and a half, Gloria made notes of the cattle shipments and payments. When she was finished, she stared at the list and nodded in satisfaction.

Gloria scooped up the cell from the bed, hit speed dial, then waited for Dave to answer.

One concussion on top of another did little for Nash's temper, not to mention his health. He and Werner had been secured inside a shed while the rest of the unloading continued.

The truck had already left, that much Nash was certain of. What he didn't know was how long ago it had gone. The one thing he couldn't be sure about was how much time had elapsed since he'd been placed in the shed. He looked over at Werner. He could just see the young German in the false light spilling through the cracks in the shed from the floodlight outside near the stockyards. "You OK?"

"I think so," he replied.

"How long have we been in here?"

"I'm not sure, a couple of hours."

The sound of voices talking outside and the crunch of boots on gravel got louder as they got closer. Within moments, the door of the shed was unlocked and wrenched open, two men standing in the void.

"Get up," Olsen snarled. "Get up or I'll damn well kick you up."

Both Werner and Nash climbed to their feet, Nash, a little unsteady, but his head soon cleared of the fog. "Where are we going?" Nash asked.

"Just shut up and move."

It took a moment to realize, but the other person with Olsen was Smith. The two of them were marched across the open ground of the homestead yard and into the house itself. Once inside, they found Moffat in the kitchen with Knackers Ellis.

Moffat's eyes narrowed. "What the fuck were you doing out prowling around tonight when you're meant to be in your room?"

Nash said, "Like I told Brutus here, I was having a piss behind the shed."

"He doesn't believe you. Neither do I. So, unless you can come up with another excuse, I have to figure out what to do with you. Both of you."

The private investigator knew what that meant. They would be lucky to see the light of day. Well, may as well put the wind up them and see how they react.

"That would be a bad idea," Nash said confidently.

"Why is that?" Olsen sneered.

"Because if I disappear then you'll have police so far up your ass that you'll feel their knobs massaging the back of your throat."

"What?" Moffat asked.

"I'm an undercover working for the Western Australia police. If they don't hear from me, they'll swarm this place like bees around a queen."

Olsen and Moffat looked at each other, not sure what to make of it.

"Bullshit," Ellis said. "I know cops, and you ain't one."

"Really? We know all about this operation. This place is a waystation for cattle shipments. You hold the stolen stock here for a week or so before sending them on to get slaughtered at the meat works that Olsen's uncle owns."

"How the fuck does he know that?" Moffat growled at Olsen.

"He can't," Olsen said.

"Well, it sure doesn't sound like it."

Nash stared at Moffat. He looked as though he was the one to crack first. "Then there was the body I found the other day."

"What about it?"

"You don't think I would just find something like that and let it go, do you? It had ID on it. The body was a missing kid called Rory Williams. Went missing with a girl called Tiffany." He almost added Nash but pulled himself up. It could have blown it all apart.

"Shit, this is bad," Moffat said.

"We have to make him disappear," Olsen said.

"I agree," said Ellis.

"Haven't you two been listening?" Moffat asked. "The cops know."

"We've only got his word for it. Even so, if they can't find him, they've got nothing."

"I don't like it. Where do you suppose we get rid of the

body?"

"The caves. It's twenty kilometers from here."

"It's still on the damn station."

"Yeah, but that's why it's a good place."

"What if the police come looking?"

"They're not going to go over this place with a fine-toothed comb. All we need to do is make a couple of calls and we can seed a false trail like he left."

"I still don't like it."

"Yeah, well it's all we got."

"What about the kraut?" Ellis asked.

"Put him in there, too."

"I'd like to know where his root went; she was a good fuck and all."

Nash looked for a reaction but there wasn't one. Instead, Olsen said, "She probably got sick of your limp dick and pissed off. Now, are you going to do it, or do you want me to?"

"I will," Ellis said with a smile.

"Take Smith with you. It's about time he got his hands dirty. And don't stuff it up."

Nash stared at the wall. Olsen had just given them a way out without even realizing it.

"In the morning," Moffat said, "I want all the backpackers off this damn place."

"What for?" Olsen asked.

"If the cops do come sniffing around, they won't have anyone other than the regular hands to talk to. No slipups that way."

"All right, I'll see to it."

Moffat stared at Nash with uncertainty. "If you thought that piece of information was going to save you, you were mistaken, Nash. If that is your real name."

Nash nodded. "Dave Nash."

"Whatever, it doesn't matter a shit now. Get rid of them."

"We're what?" Smith asked incredulously.

"You heard," snapped Ellis. "We're taking them out to the caves and killing them."

"Why me?" the young hand pleaded.

"The boss figured it was time for you to pull your weight."

Smith glanced at Nash who nodded at him. "All right."

They loaded Nash and Werner into the back of an 80 series Land Cruiser and started the journey to the caves.

The road was rough, full of corrugations that would rattle a man's back teeth out and shatter the rest. The vehicle was old and had been abused. The tail shaft vibrated something fierce and so did a hundred other things.

Nash listened for any indication of what was happening between the two men sitting in the front. At one point he heard Smith ask, "Are you going to do it?"

"The fuck. We do one each. Which one do you want?"

"None."

"Stiff shit, mate. I tell you what, I'll do the German."

"All right."

"You haven't seen his root around, have you? It's like she disappeared. One moment she was hot for it and then she just vanished."

"No."

"She was a goer, mate. Let me tell you. I had her bent over behind the machinery shed the other day and I thought she would rip the iron off it. Then when she'd had enough, she got down on her knees and—"

"All right, I get the picture," Smith said.

"Suck a golf ball through a vacuum cleaner hose she would."

"I get it, I said," the young hand shot back at him.

"What's with you?" Ellis asked. "It isn't like you haven't screwed one of the backpackers before."

"I didn't go on and on about it either."

"Whatever."

They drove on in silence and Nash lost all track of time. When the vehicle finally stopped, the sun was rising in the east and there was a freshness to the red landscape around them.

They got the two prisoners out of the vehicle and stood them away from it just in case there was blood spatter. Nobody wanted to wash it. "Get the rifle out of the Cruiser," Ellis ordered Smith.

He turned and opened the front passenger door, retrieving the weapon. Werner looked at Nash, concern and fear etched deep in his face. "It's all right," Nash said to him.

Smith got the rifle and worked the bolt, putting a round in the chamber. Then before Ellis could react, he swung the rifle in his direction and fired.

Ellis crumpled to the ground as the bullet ripped through his body, tearing apart all it touched. Beside Nash, Werner gasped in shock, unsure of what was happening or what he'd just witnessed.

"Get me untied, Terry."

The young man stepped forward and released the bonds with trembling hands. "I—I couldn't let him kill you."

Nash patted him on the shoulder and took the rifle from him. "You did what you had to do. Untie Werner."

"What are we going to do now?" Smith asked.

"I've got unfinished business with Moffat and Olsen," Nash said. He took out his cell.

"Waste of time," Smith said. "Unless you have a sat phone you get nothing."

"Are there any other stations out this way?"

"No. The closest is Moffat homestead."

"Then we'll go with what we have and work it from there."

MEEKATHARRA
WESTERN AUSTRALIA

"Gloria Browning?" the woman asked when Gloria opened the door.

Gloria looked at her watch. It was just after 6am. "That's right."

"I'm Detective Constable Gerri Tyson."

Tyson obviously worked out, looking fit. Her dark hair was in a ponytail, and she wore little if any makeup. "Pleased to meet you. I'll just get my bag."

"Yes, ma'am."

Gloria retrieved her handbag from the bed and walked back to the door where Tyson waited patiently. Inside it was the ledger from her raid the night before. "Are we headed directly back to Mount Warrigal?"

"Yes, ma'am. I have instructions to take you to the police station there."

"Fine, let's go."

They climbed into the unmarked car and Tyson reversed from the park. Once out on the street she turned left onto the highway and started their journey.

The road was surrounded by a coppery red landscape dotted with the dull green of sparse scrub.

"You're not from WA?" Tyson said. It was more of a statement than a question.

Gloria shook her head. "No. Emerald in Queensland."

"Been to Queensland a couple of times," the detective replied. "Went to Gympie for the Muster. Pissed down rain."

"Never been," Gloria said. "Maybe one day. How long have you been a D?"

"Just over three years. What about you? How long have you been a copper?"

Gloria blew out a long breath. "I've been with the QPF for around 12 months. Before that I ran an undercover taskforce for the Feds. Before that I was a UC."

"Whoa, you've been around then."

"You could say that."

"What made you get out?" Tyson asked as they blew past

the Meekatharra sign on the way out of town.

"Two of the most amazing people I know."

"Really?"

"Yes. Their names are Rachel and Dave."

"Rachel?"

"Yes, she's my daughter. Takes after her father, although he would argue that there was more of me in her." Gloria felt a surge of pride just talking about her daughter.

"Dave your husband?"

Gloria grinned just picturing Nash's face if he heard the word husband. "Partner. We worked together some before we got out at the same time."

"Wait, is he the bloke who is out at Moffat Station?"

"Yes."

"Everyone is talking about him," Tyson said. She saw the alarm on Gloria's face. "No, nothing that will compromise him. Just about his exploits and stuff. Is it true about what happened in Victoria?"

"Which part?"

"About him shooting those people because they killed one of his own?"

Killed one of my own. "Yes."

"And that he took on the Griffith Mafia?"

We took on the Griffith Mafia. "Yes."

"What's he like?"

Careful dear, you're gushing. "He's just a normal man."

"Really? I find that hard to believe."

"Really. He smells, doesn't pick up after himself, can only cook on a barbecue, leaves the toilet seat up, leaves his clothes on the floor, lasts two minutes in bed, and thinks only of himself. However, he is a good father. Was your father a copper?"

"Yes."

"Figures. A lot of times the career is a family affair. Mine too."

The conversation dried up for a while as they drove on. The silence was broken once again by Tyson. "Why do you need protection?"

The question surprised Gloria. "Didn't they tell you?"

"No. I'm only a lowly detective constable."

"A woman has sent a hit man after Nash."

Tyson frowned. "Wait, is this the same person who—"

"Yes."

"Shit."

Thirty minutes later, things changed, starting with a blue Commodore parked on the side of the highway and a man lying beside it.

Tyson slowed the unmarked car to a stop. Both women stared at the body on the asphalt. It was Gloria who spoke. "I don't like it."

"What is it you don't like?" Tyson asked.

"It just feels off."

Tyson took her sidearm from her holster and reached for the door handle.

"You should call it in," Gloria said.

"After I check it out."

She climbed out of the vehicle and closed the door. Gloria muttered a curse under her breath and reached over into the back seat for her bag. She opened the zipper and took out the Glock, making sure there was a round in the chamber.

Meanwhile, Tyson moved slowly towards the prone figure on the highway, her weapon down at her side. Gloria watched anxiously as the detective constable took each step. Subconsciously she reached for the door handle, using it to crack the door.

Tyson closed the gap between herself and the man on the asphalt, her breathing heavy, her heartbeat loud. Every step she heard the crunch of grit beneath her shoes.

Finally, she stopped. The man who lay at his feet seemed fine with no obvious signs of trauma. But as she started to bend over to check his pulse, he moved. Not just slightly, but a surge of power as he rolled over, his right arm straightening, the gun in his fist pointed straight at her.

Tyson reeled back reflexively, squeezing the trigger of her weapon. The bullet ricocheted off the road, disappearing into the desert. The man, however, didn't flinch as he squeezed the trigger of his own weapon twice.

Tyson staggered back, a gasp escaping her lips. She sat down hard on the asphalt, trying to comprehend what had just happened. The man rose stiffly to his knees and shot her once more in the chest, the force of the round slamming her back.

Gloria watched on in horror from inside the car. She

hesitated but a moment before flinging the door wide, then coming out of her seat. She fired three times at the man who was still down on the road. All the shots missed, giving him a chance to return fire.

Joe Black was surprised at what had just happened. Of all the things and cars and people that he could meet out here, suddenly he was faced with police. It had to be police. It couldn't be anyone else.

He fired once as he came up onto his knees but knew instantly that the bullet had flown wide. The blonde woman standing behind the door fired again, forcing him to roll away to the right. He felt one of the rounds tug at his jeans as he moved, lucky though it didn't find flesh.

Grinding his teeth against the pain of movement, Black blew off half a magazine at the vehicle, seeing the glass in the passenger window disintegrate and holes punch through the thin skin of the door.

Gloria dived inside the vehicle to escape the savage fusillade. Cursing, she ducked down, then leaned out a bit, her hand raised in the air, firing her weapon in the general direction of the man who was trying to kill her.

Her Glock slide stayed back as a magazine emptied. She brought it back in, dropped out the magazine, and reached in her pocket for a fresh one. Meanwhile, Black opened fire again and this time holes punched through the front windshield before it eventually gave way and rained down upon her in small cubes of glass.

"Motherfucker!" Gloria exclaimed and fired back.

She heard a cry of pain and saw the man lunge behind his vehicle, which was parked on the side of the highway. Gloria fired another three rounds after him, knowing full well that they had only hit the vehicle he was now sheltering behind.

Gloria reached for her cell to make an emergency call. There was no signal, no anything. She flung the phone to the floor and reached for the vehicle's radio. As her hand reached out, a hail of bullets rained down upon the vehicle as though a storm had opened overhead.

The radio exploded and bullets punched into the seat above her head as well as through the dash. Gloria felt the burn of a bullet graze her skin, taking flesh with it as it passed. Outside, she could hear the rat-tat-tat-tat of an automatic weapon. The prick had a fucking machine gun.

Gloria threw herself from the vehicle as more rounds punched through its flimsy exterior. Quickly, she scrambled around to the rear, placing the engine block between herself and the shooter.

Gloria dropped out the magazine of the Glock to check the rounds. She then patted her pocket to feel the reassuring shape of—if insufficient—her final full magazine. She glanced at her left arm and saw the bright red blood glisten as it ran from the open furrow in the flesh. Up until then it didn't really hurt. That changed as she looked at the torn flesh.

"Fuck."

Gloria came up and fired once more, twice, her bullets

punching into the vehicle the shooter was behind. She was a woman with a handgun in a fight against an automatic weapon. She was screwed unless something happened to tip the scales her way.

So she stopped shooting, waiting for another burst of fire from her assailant, lay flat so she could see under the vehicle.

Then she waited.

Gloria had no idea how long she lay there. Two, five minutes. Nor had she any idea what the shooter was doing. What gave him away was the sound of boots on gravel. He'd circled wide around instead of coming straight on and in doing so, was now behind her.

She tensed, waiting for him to get closer. The footsteps were still audible, but she remained still trying to regulate the rise and fall of her chest, even though she was still on her front.

At least a couple minutes elapsed as she listened to the footsteps coming closer, the crunching louder. She could hear the breathing. It sounded heavy, labored. It seemed like there was a wet rattle coming from deep within.

One more footstep, just one more. Crunch.

Gloria rolled onto her back, bringing up the Glock. A surprised expression was etched on Joe Black's face as he suddenly realized he'd made a fatal error. Gloria just had time to recognize the wet patch on his shirt, before pulling the trigger three times.

The big man was rocked back on his heels, staggering under the impact of each blow. His jaw dropped, his mouth agape as shock set in. Gloria took time to aim her fourth round before squeezing the trigger. This one, even though it hit him in the chest, put him down.

"Eat that, motherfucker."

With her chest rising and falling rapidly, drawing in huge gulps of air, Gloria came to her feet. She kept the handgun pointed at the man on the ground, even though he was unmoving.

Gloria kicked the M4 carbine out of reach, just in case even an ounce of life remained in him. Then she knelt down, resting her knee beside him, checking for a pulse. There was nothing, Black was dead.

She went through his pockets and found three drivers' licenses and a bundle of cash. In another pocket were two cell phones. One was a burner, the other looked to be a personal one.

She opened the call log on it by using the fingerprint recognition and looked through it, picking out the one he'd called most and hit dial. Nothing happened.

Gloria stuffed it in her pocket, along with the other one.

Next, she walked over to check on Tyson, even though she knew she was dead. The young detective constable stared up at the blue sky with sightless eyes, and Gloria shook her head. "Fucking asshole."

She turned and walked back to the police car, sat in on the passenger seat and reached for the transmitter for the radio. But it was futile; the radio was screwed. She threw the handset at the dash and then cursed once more.

Suddenly Gloria heard a revving engine. She looked up through the space where the windscreen used to be and saw a white Land Cruiser tray back coming towards her position. She climbed out and stood in the middle of the road and waved the driver down.

He pulled up and stared at her. She said, "I need your help."

CHAPTER SEVENTEEN

MOFFAT STATION

The vehicle came to a stop around two kilometers from the main homestead. Nash took the rifle and some spare ammunition and got out. "You two go somewhere and find a phone, call it in to the police, tell them to get out here as soon as possible."

"What are you going to do?" Smith asked.

"I'm going to put a stop to it, somehow."

"On your own?"

"I work better alone," Nash said. "I'm used to it."

"Let me come with you," Smith said.

"No. The less I have to worry about, the better. When you make the phone call, ask for Detective Inspector Len Miller. He'll know what to do."

Smith nodded. "Detective Inspector Len Miller, got it."

"What about Emma?" Werner asked. "Try to find her."

"If she's here, I will, but I doubt that she is."

"But you will try?"

"Yes, I will try."

Nash closed the door and Smith put the vehicle in gear before driving off, a cloud of dust trailing behind it. The private investigator looked in front of him at the terrain. It was scattered with lumps of grass and red ironstone gravel. He set out walking towards the homestead through the sparse scrub.

It took Nash half an hour to reach the outskirts of the homestead. As he approached, he made sure that one of the large machinery sheds was between him and the house itself. The first thing he noticed from his position was that all the backpackers had gone. The only individuals around the homestead were the old hands, the ones that were in deep with the cattle rustling ring.

In the middle of the yard stood a 44-gallon drum with smoke and flames coming up out of it. One of the hands standing beside it, while another one approached carrying an armful of paperwork.

Nash watched as the addition of the paper sent a big puff of gray-black smoke skyward. It was obvious that they were burning everything incriminating before the police got here, covering their tracks. It was then that the private investigator realized something. There was only two there. The others were gone.

Nash stepped out from behind the machinery shed, the rifle level. "That'll do. For the moment, you blokes."

The pair spun to face him, surprised looks on their faces. Their jaws dropped at the sight of the man with the rifle. "What the hell are you doing here?" one of them asked.

"Figured I'd see if I could get my old job back," Nash told him.

"Where's Ellis and Smith?"

"Smith is on his way to make a phone call to get the police out here," Nash explained. "Ellis, on the other hand, is probably saying hi to the devil."

"Wait!" the second man exclaimed. "You're not going to shoot us, are you?"

"Not if you cooperate. Where's the rest of them?"

"They've taken the cattle out to the back sixty," the first man said.

"What's out there?" Nash asked.

"It's canyon country, plenty of places to hide the cattle out there where nobody will find them."

"How far?"

"About ten kilometers southwest. The cattle that came in last night, they managed to load them back onto the truck. They'll use that to take them most of the way."

"What about the others? The ones that are still in the other paddock?"

"That was them."

"Fine, come with me."

He took them over to the machinery shed and tied them up. "That should hold you until the police get here."

Nash jogged around the back of the shed to where his car was parked. It was there but he needed keys. "Shit."

He continued his rapid pace across to the bunkhouse and opened the door to the room where he had been staying. His stuff was gone. "Well, I won't be taking the car."

Nash walked back out into the yard and looked around. It was then he noticed a Honda trail bike. Hurrying across to it he checked the fuel tank. It was full of gas.

Slinging the rifle across his shoulder by the strap he mounted the bike, turned the key, which was still in the ignition, and kicked it over. After two goes the bike roared to life.

Nash put it in gear, opened the throttle, and dropped the clutch, letting the rear wheel spin as it shot forward, a rooster tail of dirt and dust rising behind it.

The Canyon country seemed to rise out of the desert like giant teeth from a skull. Large ironstone rocks were covered with trees and scrub growing from deep crevices that caught water when it rained. If it rained.

The trail bike danced across the rocky desert, dodging small tussocks of grass, which spelled danger should the front wheel clip them. He'd left the track some five kilometers back, thinking that he'd be quicker going across country. Now, as he dodged a low branch of a tree, he was reconsidering the wisdom of his decision.

The more he neared the canyon country, the larger the teeth seemed to be. As the bike flew over a small mound, the trail cut back across in front of him. He turned hard left, the rear tire sliding out before the bike straightened as he started to follow the worn track.

"Fark!" Nash exclaimed. He lifted his legs swiftly as a long brown serpent stretched out across the trail rose angrily at the intrusion.

The front wheel found a soft patch in the sand and gravel giving Nash cause to panic. But he held his cool, and as the bike went over the top of the snake, he prayed that it wouldn't wrap around the wheel or the forks, giving it an opportunity to strike at him.

As luck would have it, that scenario didn't eventuate, and Nash was able to regain control of the bike and open the throttle up further as he sped along the track.

After another few kilometers the track straightened out and set a course for a notch in the ironstone wall before him.

Nash slowed down. An innate sense within him told him that all wasn't right. His fears were realized when a bullet streaked out of the outback heat, smashing into the front of the bike causing it to wobble erratically before going down.

Nash ground his teeth as he braced for impact, feeling stones and gravel bite into flesh as he slid along, hot on the tail of the sliding bike. No sooner had he stopped when he was up and running, snarling as the pain from his cuts and grazes scored his nerve endings.

The PI dropped behind a large ironstone boulder and grimaced. He unslung the rifle, checked it, then looked himself over quickly. His pants and shirt were torn, and patches of blood were showing through the dark dust. "Shitting bastard," Nash growled.

He raised the rifle and eased around the corner of the boulder, looking to pinpoint the location of the shot's origin.

The sound of a crack followed by a high-pitched whine as a bullet spanged off the boulder and ricocheted out into the desert. Nash swore and leaned back behind cover, bringing the rifle up to use the scope.

The shot had given him a general idea of the shooter's position, but he needed to be sure. The thing he couldn't work out was why the shooter was even there.

Another shot hit almost the same place as the last, but this time Nash held his nerve. He saw where the shooter was, a shelf of rock, lying flat where he could see the approaches.

Nash ducked back and moved around the other side of the boulder before the shooter could fire again. He needed to change his position for a clearer field of fire. He broke cover and ran towards a nearby clump of rocks. There was no gunfire, so Nash figured he'd gotten there unseen.

Once again, the rifle came up and he edged around the rock he was using for cover. He nestled his eye in behind the scope then hoped it hadn't been too knocked around from the stack he'd taken off the bike.

Nash lowered it and turned the dials on the side and top then brought it back up. He could see the shooter atop his rock, searching for him. The PI adjusted his aim, let out a slow breath, and squeezed the trigger.

The rifle slammed back against Nash's shoulder as the projectile exploded from the barrel at 3,200 feet per second—and missed.

"Motherf—" Nash growled under his breath as he worked the bolt. "Useless prick."

He leaned back out and steadied the rifle but when he looked through the scope, the shooter was gone.

Nash swept the rock ledge looking for any sign of the man and saw nothing but a rock wallaby bounding away from an overhang where it had been trying to stay out of the heat.

"Bloody hell," Nash muttered and broke cover moving to his right and forward.

The PI stopped behind the thick butt of a gum tree and paused before moving again, this time back to his left, but keeping the forward movement.

More rocks and trees but no gunfire. Soon Nash was under the line of sight from above and at the base of the escarpment. He then slung the rifle and started to climb.

CHAPTER EIGHTEEN

**MOUNT WARRIGAL
WESTERN AUSTRALIA**

"I want everybody out there in those bloody vehicles, now," Detective Inspector Len Miller barked. "I want to see nothing but asses on the way out that door."

Since the phone call, the station had been a hive of panicked activity. Sergeant Ralph Halliday had brought in his people as well, now all wore body armor, and some carried shotguns as well. He looked at Miller. "You and your people follow me."

Miller nodded and was about to run out the door when his cell rang. He answered it saying, "Make it quick, I've got a situation—"

He seemed to stop midstride. "Fuck me. Speak."

A couple of minutes later he emerged, looked around the vehicles, and spotted Halliday. "Ralph!"

Halliday jogged over. "What is it?"

"The shit has just totally hit the fucking fan. Do you have enough manpower to go out to Moffat Station?"

Halliday looked around. He had Parker and another officer. "There are three of us."

"I'll give you Harvey, will that do?"

"I guess it'll have to," Halliday replied. "Listen, what the hell is going on?"

"I've got another dead cop and Gloria Browning is missing."

"Christ."

"Yeah, and that's putting it mildly. Whatever you do, don't tell Nash until I get back to you."

"Understood."

"Just secure everything out at Moffat and get in touch when it's done. I'll reach out to Rural Crimes and have them fly some people up as soon as possible. This damn thing is a pile of shit that's way out of control. One dead copper is too many, but right now we've got at least two, maybe three. I don't want any more. Be careful."

"Count on it."

Minutes later, they were going their separate ways.

Harvey sat up front beside Halliday in a Nissan Patrol. Behind them came Parker and Johnson in a second Patrol. "Did Miller say much before he left?"

"No, not at all. Just that we had an officer down."

"Shit, don't it ever stop?"

When they arrived at the station, they found the two men tied at the machinery shed where Nash had left them. Smith and Werner made their presence known soon after the police arrived.

"Where's Nash?" Harvey snapped at them.

"No idea," Smith replied. "He should be here."

Harvey looked at the two hands being pushed by Parker and Johnson towards the second of the pair of police vehicles.

"Wait up," Harvey said. "You two. Who tied you up?"

"No one," the first replied.

"You just fucking did it to yourselves, huh?"

"Something like that."

Harvey stepped forward and punched him in the stomach, doubling him over. "Try again, shithead."

"Fu—fu—fuck you," the hand eventually managed, spittle dribbling from his lips.

The detective focused on the second of the two men. "What about you, assclown?"

"Get f—"

The hand choked on his words as Harvey hit him like his friend. The man doubled over, retching, coughing, trying to regain his breath.

"Hey!" Halliday barked. "Get off. This isn't how we do things here."

The sergeant's glare met Harvey's and the two remained locked for a moment before Harvey snarled, "Then what the shit do you propose?"

Halliday turned to the two men. "Where is he?"

"Out in the canyon country."

"Why did he go out there?"

"He's crazy. He wants to kill Olsen."

"Why?" Halliday asked.

"Like I said, he's crazy," the hand replied.

"What are they doing out there, anyway?"

"Looking for strays."

"Trying to hide stolen cattle more like," Smith said.

The hand's face screwed up. "What the fuck would you know, asshole?"

"All right, that's enough. Detective Harvey and I'll go out there. Johnson, you and Parker sit on these guys until we sort this out."

"I'll come with you," Smith said.

"No, you stay here."

"But—"

"He's right," Harvey said. "You stay."

The two men climbed into the 4X4. Halliday started the engine and engaged the transmission. As the vehicle lurched forward, Harvey turned to him and said, "Do you know where we're going?"

"Yeah, I know."

THE CANYONS

Nash clawed his way over the rim and took a knee before unslinging the rifle. He raised it and looked through the scope, sweeping the plateau he was on. It wasn't big by any stretch and beyond it were heaving undulations from a million years ago when the canyon country had been formed. Now it was covered with trees, scrub, and ironstone rock.

Nash stopped his track and threw himself sideways just as the rifle from the shooter fired. The bullet cracked as it passed overhead, cutting through the air where he'd been moments before. He'd been lucky, if the scope had been moving any faster, he would have missed the man altogether and been killed.

Nash brought the rifle up and looked through the scope once more. He found his target and fired. He saw the shooter lurch and disappear.

The PI came to his feet and ran forward, careful not to stay in a straight line for too long. Not that it mattered, the man was dead. It was one of the hands he'd seen around the station. Obviously, a lookout just in case the police were coming.

Continuing across the plateau, Nash came to the edge where it dropped away, sloping towards the canyon floor where he saw an empty cattle truck below. With no ramp or yards, they would have jumped them off. However, there were no beeves in sight, either. They had to be further in, preferably somewhere there was enough water.

Instead of cresting the edge and dropping down into the canyon, Nash jogged north along the rim towards where the gorge bent around to the left. He stopped and knelt, looking along the vacant fissure. He brought the rifle up, using the scope to look closer.

Tracks and cow shit.

"Well, no need to guess which way they went."

Staying atop the plateau he continued circling around until he came to a fork in the canyon. Nash stopped and once more used the scope to look at the trail. They had taken the left one which meant he needed to descend from his current position in order to follow it.

He was about to do so when a police vehicle appeared. To get where it was it had to have driven past the truck, yet it had failed to stop and check it out.

Nash frowned.

The doors opened and two people climbed out. Halliday and Harvey.

Harvey walked forward, looking at the churned-up ground. "You were right, they went this way."

"I had a feeling they might," Halliday replied.

Harvey turned. "What I want to know is why you didn't stop and check out the truck?"

Halliday's sidearm was already out. It came up and pointed at the detective's middle. "I kind of figured you would ask that."

"You're part of it too, huh?" Harvey said. "Should have guessed, a big operation like this."

"What can I say, the pension just won't be enough."

"So you screw your colleagues over for a few extra dollars."

"Not true. I had a choice. Choose what I was already getting or a little extra."

"Yeah. I think I know what you chose."

"It's nothing personal."

Harvey's face grew red with anger. "The fuck it isn't. It's all personal. You won't get away with this. Miller is good at his job. He'll nail you to a wall when it's all over."

"We'll see."

Then his finger began to tighten on the trigger.

Harvey jumped when the shot came. The report seemed to echo along the canyon, bouncing off the walls. However, there was no pain, just a high-pitched scream of unbearable agony.

Halliday was down, his right leg bloody, the bone shattered by the passage of the bullet. The noise emitted by the copper was shrill and deafening as he grasped at his wounded leg trying to force the pain away. Beside him lay his discarded police weapon.

Harvey lunged forward and scooped it up before looking around to see where the shot had come from. It was then he saw Nash climbing down the side of the gorge towards him.

"Help me," Halliday whimpered. "I'm shot."

"Shut the fuck up."

Harvey turned to greet Nash. "Good thing you came along when you did. Thanks."

Nash nodded. "I was warned about the police when I arrived."

"You figure the others are in on it?"

The PI stared at Halliday. "Let's find out."

Walking up next to Halliday, he kicked him in the wounded leg, getting blood on his boot, almost causing the corrupt cop to pass out with pain. Examining the man's leg, he then leaned down and grabbed a handful of hair, turning the sweat-streaked face upward. "Who else is in on it? Parker? Your other constable?"

"N—no."

"Just you?"

"Y—yes. Get me s—some help."

"Where have they taken the cattle?" Nash asked.

"To the billabong."

"What billabong?"

"You'll f—find it. Can't miss. Now help me." His words came out in a hiss as he gave a painful grimace.

Nash leaned down to Halliday's belt and removed his handcuffs, using them to restrain him. Halliday looked bewildered. "What are you doing? I need medical help."

"You'll get it; eventually."

The police sergeant's face took on a nasty expression. "Fuck you, Nash. We should have fucking killed you when you came to town, but he thought it better to keep an eye on you. Thought you'd just go away. But no."

"*He* knew?"

"Of course, he fucking knew. Then your bitch turned up."

"Who is he, Halliday?"

"Byron Willis."

"He knows about Gloria?" Nash asked.

"Isn't that what I just said?" Halliday growled. "His sons get hold of her, she's screwed like the rest of them."

Nash's mind whirled. To Harvey they were just words, but to Nash they were pieces of a puzzle which were falling into place.

"Tell me about his sons, Halliday."

The copper smiled wickedly. Nash was about to kick him when Harvey said, "We don't have time, Nash. We've got other business to attend to."

"You heard what the prick said," Nash shot back at him.

"I did, but I can't get these people on my own."

"Fuck," Nash snarled. "Come on then."

THE HIGHWAY SOUTH OF MEEKATHARRA

"What the hell do we have?" Miller asked looking at the still-covered bodies on the highway.

The senior detective in charge ran him through what he knew and his theory. "They stopped over there. Tyson got out of the vehicle and came forward to here. Why? I have no idea, maybe she was lured. The other woman—"

"Browning."

"Browning remained in the vehicle. Black shot Tyson and then he started firing at Browning. Somewhere in the fight he changed his weapon over to an assault rifle."

"So the dead guy is our man?"

"Yes. Judging by the way he's knocked around he was the same guy who went out the window at the hotel."

"Browning shot him?" Miller asked as he started walking towards the second body.

"We assume so. Black circled around trying to get in behind her. The only reason I can think of why he'd do that is because he thought she was hit. Maybe she lured him in with his own trick."

"Good on her."

Miller looked around. "Tell me what happened to Browning?"

"We don't know. It's like she just vanished." He pointed at the handgun on the asphalt with a tag next to it. "We assume that's hers."

Miller frowned. "So, our suspect hits them, then Browning kills him, then someone comes along and takes her."

"That's about it."

Miller pointed at another tag not far away with the number fifty-five on it. "Blood?"

"Yeah, it's more than likely hers."

"Shit."

"Not enough to be fatal so we have to assume that she's still alive."

Miller shook his head. "Where the hell is she then?"

MOFFAT STATION

Nash looked through the scope at the scene before them. The cattle were milling around the billabong which in turn was partially enclosed by gums and scrub. He could easily make out Olsen off to one side talking on a satellite phone. Beside him stood Moffat. Four other hands were talking amongst themselves, it looked as though the truck driver was also with them.

Olsen disconnected the call and instantly turned to face Moffat, lifting the rifle he was carrying, and shot him down.

"Shit a brick," hissed Harvey.

"What do you want to do?" he asked Harvey.

"Can't call for backup."

"Nope."

"Too many to go down there and try to arrest."

"Yeah."

"How good are you with that rifle?"

"Fair. Are you asking me to shoot someone?" Nash said.

"No. Can you stampede the cattle?"

"Maybe. Someone might get hurt though."

Harvey shrugged. "I think we're beyond that. Shouldn't steal cattle. Dangerous occupation."

"You're the boss."

Nash brought the weapon up to his shoulder and looked through the scope. He sighted on the target he wanted and took a deep breath before letting it out slowly.

The rifle slammed back against his shoulder, the roar bouncing off the ironstone rocks. Even as the bullet hit at the feet of the already skittish cattle, Nash was working the bolt.

It only took another two shots to get the herd moving. Panicked moans rose in crescendo until they stopped milling and one beast broke from the group. The rest followed.

Men scattered, and amongst the carnage Nash saw a rider on a bike go down and within moments was swept under the surging mass.

The rest of the hands scattered like leaves in the wind. Nash fired again and the cattle picked up speed.

Trying to locate Olsen amongst the herd and dust cloud

which roiled into the air was fruitless. Soon the dust cloud was so big that everything was enveloped and disappeared beneath it.

"There's another one over here," Nash said to Harvey as they walked towards the billabong. It was the second crushed body they'd discovered since the dust cloud and cattle had gone.

"Yeah, I got one over here, too," the detective replied.

"Your boss is going to love this."

"Leave it to me. Do you see your friend Olsen anywhere?"

"Not yet."

"Maybe the slippery bastard—"

BLAM!

Harvey buckled at the knees and went down as the sound of the shot shattered the serenity. Nash whirled and saw Olsen, or what was left of Olsen, lurching towards him, a rifle in his hands.

He was dragging his right leg, his shirt was torn, and blood covered his face. Judging by the way his breathing was labored, his chest was stove in as well.

Nash never thought about his next movements, he just let his instincts take over. The rifle roared and the bullet punched into Olsen, hard. The foreman went down and never moved. The PI knew he was dead so ignored him and went to Harvey's side.

The detective was dying, no two ways about it. "I need to

go somewhere where I can get reception to call an ambulance."

"Don't bother. I'm dying. I can feel it. But before I do, there's something you need to know."

"Just rest," Nash said. "Let me get some help."

"Your woman has disappeared."

Nash froze. "What do you mean?"

Harvey spoke again, this time. His voice was softer. "Joe Black hit their car. Killed the constable. It looks like Gloria killed him. But then she disappeared."

"Fuck!" Nash said bitterly.

"Go. Go and find her."

Nash didn't want to leave the dying man there, but he had to find Gloria. Harvey could see the torment in his eyes. "Don't worry about me, Nash. I'll be dead soon. There's no one else."

"I'm sorry, Harvey."

"Just make sure that Miller understands everything was my idea."

"Do they know who took her?"

"I don't think so." His voice was little more than a whisper.

Nash climbed to his feet, looked around. Harvey's handgun was lying in the dirt. He picked it up and put it in the man's hand. "Just in case."

"Go find her, Nash. Fuck off."

"I'll get you some help, Harvey."

"That would be good."

Carrying the rifle, Nash jogged along the canyon until he reached where he had left Halliday. The sergeant was still obviously in pain. But Nash was beyond caring. He looked down at the wounded man. "Right, asshole, you're going to tell me everything you know. Leave nothing out."

The police four-wheel drive slid to a stop and Nash climbed out. Staring at him were both Johnson and Parker as they waited for an explanation. "Your sergeant is out at the canyons. He's been shot. Got what he deserved. He's part of it. Harvey is out there, too. He's dying. Gunshot, Olsen did it. You'll need to get an ambulance out there."

Werner and Smith appeared. "Are you all right, Nash?"

"Fine."

"What about the rest of them?" Parker asked.

"Dead or scattered to the wind. I'll explain later. Right now, I have something else to do."

The two police officers looked confused. "What do you mean?"

"My partner has been kidnapped by a killer. I'm certain of it. And right now, I'm going to get her back."

"Where?" asked Johnson. "Do you even know where to start?"

"There's an old goldmine west of here. Your boss told me if she was going to be anywhere, that's where it would be."

"What the hell are you on about?" Parker asked.

Johnson was making a radio call even as they spoke. "Byron Willis owns the meat works up north of here. He has three sons. You ever heard of Shit Head Willis?"

"Yes, who hasn't?"

"He and his brothers have been picking up girls off the highway and killing them. Hunting them like animals."

"How do you know this?"

"Halliday told me. He is Byron Willis's security in town. Willis pays him off to look the other way while the cattle shipments come through. Halliday has known about it for a while and has just done nothing."

"He told you this?"

"Yes, he did."

"Why would he admit to that?"

"Because he had no fucking choice."

Nash turned and started walking back towards the Land Cruiser.

"Wait. You can't go on your own."

"Are you going to try and stop me?"

"No, but I'll come with you."

Nash was in no mood to argue. "Then get the hell in."

CHAPTER NINETEEN

The heat inside the large shed was intense. Gloria felt the trickle of sweat running down her back and between her breasts turn into a rivulet. She was tied with her hands above her head, attached to an old block and tackle. Beside her was Emma who was tied in a similar fashion. Both women were naked. Gloria, having been there the least amount of time, hadn't been subjected to the heinous treatment already suffered by the German backpacker.

Shit Head Willis stood in front of Gloria, licking his lips. He reached out and tweaked a nipple and grinned sickeningly as it hardened.

"You like that, bitch, huh?"

"Fuck off."

"You're different to the others. I'm really going to enjoy fucking you."

"Stop playing with her, Shit Head," Paul growled, sipping on his beer. "Just do it. Screw the bitch good."

His brother shook his head. "Not yet. I want to have some fun first."

Paul threw his beer onto the floor. "Fun? I'll show you some fun. Get your rifle."

"Why?"

"Just do it."

Stewart Willis picked up his rifle. "Now what?"

"Point it at the German bitch's head and if the copper mole doesn't do what I say, fucking shoot her."

Stewart grinned. "What are you going to do, Paul?"

"Watch."

Moments later, Emma gasped as the rifle barrel was held inches from her head. Fresh tears ran from her eyes, coursing down her dust-streaked cheeks. Paul walked over to Gloria and said, "If you try anything, or don't do what I say, Shit Head will kill the bitch, understand?"

Gloria glared at him, her jaw set. The middle Willis Brother reached out and grasped Gloria's right nipple, twisting savagely, eliciting a gasp of pain. "Understand?"

She nodded.

"Good."

Paul reached up and freed Gloria's right hand, making sure to leave the left secured. Then he undid his belt and jeans, dropping them down around his knees. The sense of power he was wielding had him excited and his cock was hard.

He grabbed Gloria's hand. "Stroke it."

Gloria fought against him.

"Do it or my brother will kill her," Paul snarled.

As she worked into a rhythm, Gloria stared into the sadistic bastard's eyes. "He'll kill you."

"Who will?"

"Nash."

"Who's Nash?" He raised an eyebrow, his curiosity only half piqued, but he was too focused on what was happening to his genitalia to care much.

"Your worst fucking nightmare."

Paul chuckled and then let a moan escape his lips. "Just shut up and keep going."

Suddenly the third brother Brian appeared. "Hey, we've got a problem."

"Frig off, I'm busy," Paul growled.

"Screw that, someone is here."

"Shit," the middle Willis brother hissed, pulling himself free of Gloria's grasp and grabbing his pants to haul them up. "There's always something."

"He's here," Gloria sneered. "Now you'll find out the true definition of hell."

Paul's right hand lashed out, clipping Gloria across the jaw. She yelped in pain and her head slumped forward.

The middle brother turned to the other two. "Well, don't just stand there, go and find out who it is."

"Don't give me orders, Paul," Shit Head snarled.

Paul shook his head. "Come on, you dick."

Moments later, they had left the shed, all armed and ready.

After several seconds of silence, Gloria's head snapped up, her eyes wide and alert. She glanced across at Emma. "Are you ready?"

Emma shook her head. "I don't think I can," she sobbed.

Gloria reached up with her free hand. "Too bad, you've got no choice in the matter. If they kill Dave, we need to get away from here."

"You don't even know if it's him."

"It's him. I know it."

Nash looked at Parker from where they lay on the low ridge overlooking the old mine site. The scene below them would not be out of place in a post-apocalyptic movie. Large, rundown sheds with rusted corrugated iron exteriors. Old conveyers, disabled trucks, and other machinery. All except for the two battered Land Cruisers parked near a shed at the center of the site. "I guess we lucked onto them," Nash said.

"What do you want to do?"

"Can you use a rifle?"

Parker nodded. "I grew up on the land."

Nash's gaze grew intense. "I'm going to ask you to do something that you were told at the academy never to do. I need your Glock."

Her eyes widened. "What?"

"I'm going down there, Parker, and a rifle will be almost useless. If we trade weapons, you can cover me from up here."

"Dave, I—"

"It's the only way. They've got Gloria and I trust no one but myself to get her out of there."

"But there are three of them."

He grinned at her. "Hey, I'm Dave Nash. Haven't you heard? I'm a superhero."

Parker shook her head and reached down for her sidearm and her spare magazines. "Here. I want it back."

"You'll get it."

Nash gave her the rifle and then checked the Glock. He saw her watching him. "Habit."

She nodded, understanding.

"You ready?"

"Let's do it."

Nash came off the ridge, crouched over and using the scattered brush for cover. His main issue was the rocky slope, one misplaced step and a rolled ankle would result, limiting his mobility; something he did not need.

When he reached the foot of the slope he moved right, circling around to an old Ford dump truck, rusted, missing three wheels and windows. He crouched behind it noticing the bullet holes in its exterior.

Suddenly he heard a dog bark and cursed under his breath. Somehow the fact that these guys used dogs to hunt their victims had escaped his thought process before coming down off the ridge.

Then Nash heard the voices. Somehow, they knew he was here. So be it. If he had to go hard at them, he had no issue with that.

Nash was up and moving a few moments later. His path took him from the broken truck to a similarly wrecked conveyer. He squatted beside a small tree before moving once more towards one of the many sheds.

The PI had almost made it before a large dog, complete

with leather chest guard, came bounding out of the mine site's detritus towards him, snarling wildly.

"Christ," Nash growled and brought up the Glock. The last thing he wanted to do was shoot the dog, because it was an instrument of evil, trained to do what its masters bid. It wasn't the animal's fault.

The Glock fired twice, and dirt and rocks kicked up in front of the charging beast, spraying its face.

The animal yelped and hastily turned under the barrel of the gun which was about to fire for a third time.

Relieved, Nash changed his direction towards an old D10 dozer. He stopped in beside the metal monster's motor and listened. Wind whipped up a small dust cloud and rustled the leaves in the brush. He peered around the large steel blade and saw one of the brothers coming in his direction. It wasn't Shit Head, which meant it was one of the others. The man was armed, making him a danger that had to be put down.

Nash stepped clear of the dozer blade, weapon up. "Hold it."

Taken by surprise, the Willis Brother rode his luck a little too hard and fought to bring the rifle around. Nash calmly fired the Glock, the bullet punching into Brian Willis's chest.

The youngest of the three dropped to his knees, stunned by the sudden blow. He looked up at Nash and slowly toppled to his side to die quietly.

Shouts erupted from over near the main mine sheds. "Brian? Brian, did you get the prick?"

No answer brought more urgent shouts.

"Brian, did you get the bastard?"

"He's dead, Willis," Nash called back. "You want to give up

before you lay beside him?"

"Who the fuck are you?"

Nash tracked towards the shed he'd had his sights on earlier. "The name's Nash."

"The bitch of yours said you'd be coming. Thinks you're some kind of superman."

"She still alive, Willis?"

"For the moment. Have to have our fun with her before the hunt."

Gloria was still alive.

"Her and the German mole," Paul Willis added.

Emma?

Nash moved around the shed and found himself looking at another conveyer. He stepped out to hurry across the open ground between the shed and the structure when it happened. A loud crack and a blinding pain in his left side.

As the PI went down in a heap on the rocky ground, he knew exactly what had just happened. He'd been shot.

Gloria picked up a length of steel pipe, testing its weight in her grasp. She'd found an old pair of coveralls which she donned to cover her nakedness. They were full of holes, rotted, and had more dust and dirt than a vacuum cleaner bag, but they did their intended job. A second smaller pair she'd given to Emma.

Gloria turned to Emma. "Find a place to hide. Stay there until this is all over."

"What about you?"

"Don't worry about me. Just hide."

Emma disappeared and Gloria walked towards the door which led outside. She could feel the anger building in her. Not fear, but a deep-seated rage brought about by humiliation; if she got the chance, someone was about to pay.

Gloria squinted against the harsh glare from outside. As her eyes adjusted, she looked around. It was the first time she'd seen where they were holding her due to being blindfolded when Shit Head Willis had brought her here.

Shouted voices were audible followed by the gunshots.

More shouting followed by another shot. Then a different voice. It was Nash.

Shouts again then came the rifle shot. It was followed by, "I got him. I shot the prick."

"Oh, no."

Nash was hit hard but he was still upright on his knees. Blood ran through the fingers of his left hand, saturating his shirt. Pain radiated out from the wound, nerve endings burning like fire.

Movement in front of him drew his attention and the older Willis appeared with his rifle pointed at Nash. "Eye for an eye, asshole."

Nash had dropped the Glock when he had been shot and now there was no way he could pick it up and fire it before the oldest Willis killed him. "Shit, Gloria, I almost made it. I'm sorry."

Nash closed his eyes and waited for the end.

A rifle whiplashed and a pained grunt followed closely behind. Nash opened his eyes and saw Stewart Willis falling onto his back.

Parker.

With excruciating effort, Nash picked up the handgun and climbed to his feet. He lurched forward, each footstep barely clearing the rocky ground. He staggered past a mine shed and out into the open. Before him stood a large loader which, as had happened to the rest of the site, neglect had taken it over.

"There you are," an unfamiliar voice said.

Nash staggered as he turned to look at him. "You're next."

"What?"

"Your murdering days are over."

"Really? You don't look so well. Guess you're bleeding out really fast, mate."

Nash knew he was. He could feel it. He'd left a good trail of blood behind him which the dry earth drank greedily.

"I doubt you'll even get that gun up high enough to do the job."

"Won't have to."

"What?"

The rifle shot cracked out across the mine site. The round seemed to whistle as it came in and smashed into the killer.

Paul Willis staggered under the blow. He looked confused as he stared in bewilderment at Nash. "What the fuck?"

But all was not over for the killer. Gloria appeared with the pipe in her hands. She swung it like a pro baseballer and although the sound wasn't as loud as the rifle shot, it still echoed.

He fell face forward onto the hard ground. Gloria spat on him. "Fucking asshole."

Nash groaned and her head snapped up. "Baby?"

"Hey."

"Are you alright?"

"Nope, I'm fucked."

CHAPTER TWENTY

TWO WEEKS LATER

The press that gathered outside the Royal Perth Hospital jostled for position as Nash walked out with Gloria beside him. Questions were fired at him left and right as he was guided to the taxi which waited for them.

Nash was well and truly on the mend and couldn't wait to get home to see Rachel. Gloria was all right externally, but once she got back to Emerald the police force had her booked in for some therapy sessions.

As they sat in the back of the cab the driver said to them, "You folks kill someone?"

Something like that, Nash thought.

Paul Willis had clung to life for three days before he finally cashed in. The bullet that Parker fired had torn his insides to pieces irreparably.

Nash on the other hand had been lucky. He'd almost died from blood loss by the time he could be evacuated, but it had all worked out for him, just.

Emma had spent a week in hospital before returning to Germany.

Smith had been questioned by the police and then let go.

Werner also.

A week into his hospital recovery Miller had come to question him. It looked as though he would have to return to Perth for the inquest, but he was in the clear.

Mount Warrigal Police Station on the other hand was cleaned out and replaced with all new staff, including a sergeant.

Byron Willis was arrested the day of the shootings.

Those from Moffat Station who hadn't died in the stampede were now behind bars awaiting trial. Apart from Moffat himself who'd already been dead.

Halliday had cut himself a deal to give evidence for a reduced sentence.

Things seemed to have been tied up into a complete parcel.

A walking stick handle tapped on the glass of the taxi window beside Nash's head. "Wait," he said to the driver.

He wound the window down.

"Trying to get away without saying goodbye?" Detective Sergeant Lee Harvey asked.

"That was the idea."

By some miracle, Harvey had survived the gunshot. The doctors had expected him to die within twenty-four hours of him reaching the hospital, but there he stood, in the flesh.

"No such luck, buddy. I'll see you when you come back for the inquest."

He held out his hand and Nash took it. "I'll be here. Maybe

we can go for a beer."

"Don't forget me," Gloria said.

Harvey smiled. "Yeah, you, too. I'm looking forward to getting to know you a little more. Especially after what you did."

"Me, too," said Gloria.

"Be seeing you, Harvey," Nash said with a small salute.

"You, too, Nash. Going straight home?"

"That's the plan, but I have one stop to make along the way."

"Good luck."

The window went up and the cab pulled away from the curb. Gloria grabbed Nash's hand. "How are you feeling?"

"I'm fine."

"You know, we could go straight home. I know someone who would be very happy with that."

"I know two who'd be super happy with that. But I need to do this."

"All right."

PORT MELBOURNE WOMEN'S CORRECTIONAL FACILITY
VICTORIA

Betty O'Malley sat at the table and waited. She was unhappy about being pulled out of her cell for what was said to be visitation. She could think of no one who would come to see her.

When the door opened, her jaw dropped. Nash walked in and sat down. "Hello, Betty."

"What the feck do you want? You murdering bastard."

"Just came to show you that your little plan didn't work. Just in case you don't know, Joe Black is dead. Gloria put him in a hole."

"I don't know what you're talking about," she lied, sitting back with an innocent look on her face.

"It's alright, I know it was you. Right about now, your lawyer is being questioned by Victoria police. You should expect the extra charges over the next couple of days."

"Like I said, I don't know what you're talking about."

"And guess what? I'm going to keep my calendar clear for the trial. When you look at the gallery, I'll be sitting there in front with a big smile on my face."

Betty O'Malley's face hardened. "I'll get you, Nash. It might not be tomorrow the next day. One day you wake up and I'll have someone there who will make you pay for what you did to my sons. You'll be forever looking over your shoulder."

"Let me explain something. If you don't back off, one day you'll not wake up. You are not the only one who knows people. Have you ever heard of Ella Grainger?"

He could tell by the flicker in her eyes that she had.

"You see, Ella owes me a favor. So I'm going to get her to keep an eye on you. Anything happens or anyone sinister comes my way, I'm going to reach out. Then she is going to reach out to you. And trust me, you don't want that." Nash leaned closer to her. "So *back* off!"

"Never," she hissed.

Nash stood up. "Then good luck."

He turned and walked towards the door.

Suddenly the room was filled with the screams of Betty O'Malley.

"I'll kill you, you bastard! You're dead! Do you hear me? Dead!"

Nash went out the door, and, as he traversed the corridor, he could still hear her screaming at him.

Once outside he found Gloria waiting for him in the parking lot. She took him in her arms and held him for a time. "How did it go?"

"About as expected."

"Are you ready for home?"

Nash nodded. "Yeah, beyond ready. There's a little girl waiting for us."

"What would you say if I told you I wanted another one?"

"Another—oh, right."

"Well?"

"Only if I can name her this time."

Gloria smiled. "I'm fine with that."

"I was thinking, Vivian."

"Nash."

"Millicent?"

"Not even funny."

"Topsy?"

"Now you're just being ridiculous."

"Tiffany?"

Gloria stared at him, a tear forming in the corner of her right eye. "We can do that. But what if it's a boy?"

"Simple. We call him Dave."

A LOOK AT: DROWNING ARE THE DEAD

BEST-SELLING AUTHOR BRENT TOWNS RETURNS WITH A PRIVATE DETECTIVE MYSTERY—FULL OF SMALL-TOWN SECRECY AND DEADLY INTRIGUE.

In the middle of Australia's Outback lies the small town of Friar's Lake. It's quaint, quiet, and—more importantly—devoid of crime.

So, when a body turns up with the hallmark signs of a manic serial killer from the past, Private Investigator Trent Jacobs is hired by a town local to find out if Ten Cent—the infamous killer—is back.

But as this once-quiet town begins to unravel, tragedy strikes again, and Trent goes missing.

Thankfully, newcomer Mark Hayes is eager to help out. Until—with every shocking secret that's uncovered, he begins to question whether he can find the killer before time runs out.

After all...beneath small-town Friar Lake's dusty exterior, there are hidden truths of which even the locals are unaware.

AVAILABLE NOW

ABOUT BRENT TOWNS

A relative newcomer to the world of writing, Brent Towns self-published his first book, a western, in 2015. Last Stand in Sanctuary took him two years to write. His first hardcover book, a Black Horse Western, was published the following year.

Since then, he has written 26 western stories, including some in collaboration with British western author, Ben Bridges.

Also, he has written the novelization to the upcoming 2019 movie from One-Eyed Horse Productions, titled, Bill Tilghman and the Outlaws. Not bad for an Australian author, he thinks.

Brent Towns has also scripted three Commando Comics with another two to come.

He says, "The obvious next step for me was to venture into the world of men's action/adventure/thriller stories. Thus, Team Reaper was born."

A country town in Queensland, Australia, is where Brent lives with his wife and son.

In the past, he worked as a seaweed factory worker, a knife-hand in an abattoir, mowed lawns and tidied gardens, worked in caravan parks, and worked in the hire industry. And now, as well as writing books, Brent is a home tutor for his son doing distance education.

Brent's love of reading used to take over his life, now it's writing that does that; often sitting up until the small hours, bashing away at his tortured keyboard where he loses himself in the world of fiction.

ABOUT SAM TOWNS

Sam Towns is a mother of one, a toiler of many words, and spends most of her time fixing Brent's mistakes.

CPSIA information can be obtained
at www.ICGtesting.com
Printed in the USA
BVHW071539160922
647226BV00022B/186